SOMEBODY DIFFERENT

"Hi! I'm Maxine Grant! My family moved in about a half hour ago. When I heard voices, I just had to find out who they belonged to," this girl named Maxine said. "Hope you don't mind my barging in. My parents tell me I'm Queen of the Bargers."

Meg didn't know what to say.

"Well, Meg, you got your wish," Stevie said.

"What's that?"

Stevie grinned and pointed to the girl. "Somebody different moved next door to you. Real different."

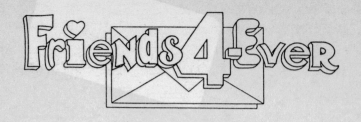

Friends 4-Ever

P.S. We'll Miss You
Yours 'Til the Meatball Bounces
2 Sweet 2 B 4-Gotten
Remember Me, When This You See
Sealed with a Hug
Friends 'Til the Ocean Waves
Friends 4-Ever Minus 1
Mysteriously Yours
C U When the Snow Falls
Yours 'Til the Wedding Rings
Best Wishes, Whoever You Are

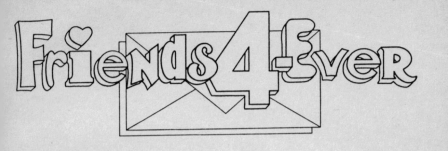

BEST WISHES, WHOEVER YOU ARE

Deirdre Corey

AN
APPLE
PAPERBACK

SCHOLASTIC INC.
New York Toronto London Auckland Sydney

ISBN 0-590-45111-1

12 11 10 9 8 7 6 5 4 3 2 1   2 3 4 5 6 7/9

Printed in the U.S.A.   28

First Scholastic printing, March 1992

To Kate Foley

BEST WISHES,
WHOEVER YOU ARE

OLD FRIENDS, BORING FRIENDS

The spying tree in front of Meg Milano's house wasn't fully leafed out yet, but it didn't matter to the four girls who were hidden in its strong branches. Down below, cars pulled out of driveways, delivery trucks came and went, and the pains-in-the-neck, Willy and Simon, played street hockey without any idea that just over-head, Meg and her three closest friends were watching everything that moved in Crispin Landing that morning. No one, not even the movers going in and out of the house next door, noticed the four pairs of dangling legs or the fact that all of them were attached to girls wearing identical dark glasses.

"I swear, these spy glasses are the neatest things," Stevie Ames said. "It's like having eyes in the back of your head with these little mirrors on the side."

"Yeah, yeah, yeah," Meg grumbled, "but what's there to see with them or these binoculars? Just a couple of birds on the roof of my house. Nothing exciting."

"What do you mean?" Molly Quindlen cried from across the tree. She pushed her chin-length brown hair behind her ears, then flipped through the notebook she had on her lap. "Listen to this, Meg: *Nine A.M. Moving van arrives. Movers take out big Ping-Pong table. Ten-thirty A.M. Van half empty. Spotted one girl's bike just like mine and same canopy bed.*" Molly stuck out her tongue at Meg, then held up the binoculars to see what else she should record in her spy notebook.

"Big deal," Meg said with bored sigh. "We could have seen all that stuff, anyway, without the I Spy Kit, just by going down there and watching."

"And miss all the fun of hiding up here, Meg? No way," Stevie protested. "Molly, hand me those, will ya? I want to get a better look at that box marked 'Sports Equipment.'"

"Wowee," Meg said in a sarcastic voice. She

2

didn't know why, but all of a sudden, the I Spy Kit her aunt Teddy had sent her for her birthday the week before seemed so babyish. What was the point of having spy glasses, binoculars, a little plastic periscope, and spy notebooks for all four of the Friends 4-Ever if there was nothing to spy on except moving boxes? "Who wants to stay out here anyway?" she asked no one in particular.

"I do, I do," Stevie answered. She reached way across her tree limb with no fear at all. "Laura, can I borrow your pencil?"

Laura tried to hand Stevie her I Spy pencil without getting her long, dark hair caught in the tree branches or losing her balance. Though she was terrified of heights, she was sure no harm could come to her when she was with the Friends 4-Ever, even twelve feet high in the air. Still, just to be safe, she hung on tightly to the tree trunk.

Stevie, on the other hand, seemed to be balanced on her branch by nothing more than the toes of her high-top sneakers. She moved around the tree branches with the ease of the squirrels who lived up there. Every part of Stevie was in motion, from her arms to her wild mop of reddish-blonde hair. With two free hands, she reached across to Laura's branch and grabbed the pencil. Then she took the binoculars from Molly and aimed them at Willy and Simon down below.

A minute later, she scribbled furiously in her spy notebook. "Those jerks! I just heard them say I cheated in the last hockey game. Why, I have a good mind to go down there and give them a — "

"Forget it," Meg said. "Unless you want them to know about our spying stuff. If they find out about it then you won't be able to spy anymore. Not that I care."

"Hey, what gives, Meg?" Molly wanted to know. "You've been begging your aunt to send you all this neat stuff since forever to solve our Clue Club mysteries. Now you're acting like somebody gave you a doll carriage by mistake."

"I wanted the I Spy Kit for my *tenth* birthday, not my eleventh!" Meg protested. "Don't you think it's a little babyish eavesdropping on Willy and Simon or spying on the movers when all they're doing is unloading boxes and boring furniture?"

Meg didn't bother to add that what she'd *really* wanted for her birthday was to be treated a little older than the year before. Somehow getting the I Spy Kit a whole year late just reminded her that *nothing* was ever going to change. Not to mention having to listen to her parents' lectures about not spying on people when they didn't know it. Now what fun was *that*?

A brisk wind blew through the tree, and Meg zipped up her bright blue windbreaker until just her forehead and her curly blonde hair were sticking out. From inside the nylon jacket she muttered to herself, "Here we are, first day of spring vacation, and what're we doing? Freezing and watching Willy and Simon, that's what!"

Laura laughed uncomfortably and tried to tease Meg out of her bad mood. "Are you talking to your jacket, Meg?"

No answer.

The I Spy Kit wasn't any fun without Meg fooling around with it, too, so Laura tried something else to get her friend to join in. "Hey, guys, it *is* freezing up here. Maybe we should go inside and plan what we're going to do on vacation."

"Don't forget the Math Marathon, either," Molly joined in. "Remember, we have all those pledges from the stores in town and people in Crispin Landing. I wish we hadn't planned to raise fifty dollars. At a nickel apiece, that's a *thousand* problems. Better get started, right, Meg?"

Still Meg didn't answer. The Math Marathon was yet another thing that seemed incredibly babyish on this sunny spring day when she wanted something to happen — something big — something different — and not just silly club things like math marathons or tree climbing or being spies up in the maple tree.

"Right, Meg?" a confused and slightly hurt Laura asked.

"Yeah, right," Meg finally answered.

"Well, I don't want to go inside," Stevie announced. "I just overheard one of the moving guys saying the new family should be here in an hour or so. Goody! When my mom sold that house to the people, she said there were two kids, a girl in high school and a girl our age. I sure hope she likes soccer, since you guys don't want to try out."

"Forget soccer," Molly reminded Stevie. "Laura and I are taking two ballet classes a week. Meg has to practice piano for the spring recital — we're just too busy. *I* just hope the new girl likes horseback riding and clubs and the Oz books, and let's see, what else?"

"Ballet," Laura said, finally letting one arm swirl through the air up and away from the safe, solid tree trunk. "What about you, Meg? What do you hope the new girl is like?"

"Different." Meg burrowed deeper into her jacket collar. "I hope she's totally different than any of us. What we need is a change."

Stevie formed a megaphone with her hands and aimed it at Meg. "WOULD YOU REPEAT THAT, PLEASE?" she said in a robotic voice. "I thought you just said we need a change. But I must have misunderstood. I mean, you're the one who always lines up all the toothbrushes so the bristles point the same way, not to mention color-coordinating your closet so that you don't get a green sweatshirt mixed in with a red one or . . ."

Unable to resist poking a little fun at the super-organized Meg Milano, Molly just had to add a couple of examples to Stevie's list. "Or how about having a spy birthday party three years in a row with the same spy burgers and the same dark glasses on top of the cake?"

At that Meg's head popped out from her jacket. "That wasn't my fault!" she protested. "I wanted to have my party at the Glitter Dome in Providence and design our own sweatshirts, but all of you kept saying how we always have to have our birthdays right here no matter what. So don't go blaming me."

Laura, who couldn't stand it when her friends squabbled, came to the rescue again. "Look, it doesn't matter what we thought. Don't you guys remember? Meg's parents wouldn't let her have her party in Providence anyway, so it was no-body's fault."

Laura's peacemaking efforts didn't help Meg feel any less cold and stiff and bored with spying on things that weren't worth spying about. "Can we go inside?" Meg asked. Without waiting for an answer she shimmied down the tree. "I don't plan to spend a whole hour out here freezing until the new family shows up."

"Well, I do!" Stevie said. She swept the bin-oculars in an arc to see what else she could spy on. "See you later."

From down on the ground, Meg heard Stevie's "Sheesh! What's with her?" and Molly's "Boy, what a grump!"

Inside the house, Meg tiptoed past her moth-er's office. But Mrs. Milano, who had eyes in the back of her head even without spy glasses, swiv-eled around and caught Meg trying to sneak by.

"Where's the rest of the group, Meg?" her mother called out.

"They're still up in the tree," Meg answered. Why didn't her mother just go back to her dental newsletter or whatever she was working on? Didn't she have anything better to do than track Meg's every footstep?

"I suppose the girls have your binoculars up there," Mrs. Milano said, though it was clear from her frown that she already knew they did. "Well, I just hope they're not spying on people."

"They're just, uh, bird-watching, Mom," Meg said.

Mrs. Milano was like a runaway train when she disapproved of something. "Really, I could just shoot Aunt Teddy for sending you all that spy gear. I tried to tell her when she called last night about the problems her gift was causing. But you know Aunt Teddy. She said she can hardly wait to try spying on the neighbors the minute Dad and I leave for the airport on Wednesday. Assuming she gets here in time, that is. Knowing Teddy, she's liable to join the circus somewhere along the way and completely forget that she promised to stay with you while Daddy and I are away."

"Talking about the black sheep of the Biddle family?" Mr. Milano had come downstairs to get an opinion on which ties to bring on the business trip they were taking. "How about this one, Meg-o?" He held up a pinkish-orange tie painted to look like a long skinny salmon, another one of Aunt Teddy's outrageous presents. "Just the thing to wear if they serve fish during one of the boring medical banquets we have to go to."

"Oh, Dad!" Meg said. She wasn't in any mood to laugh at her father's corny jokes. She was still plenty upset that her parents weren't taking her along to the medical and dental conventions in Canada that they were going to attend over the next couple of weeks.

Mr. Milano chucked Meg's chin. "C'mon, Meg-o. You still mad you're not going? I'll make sure Mom brings back a giant plastic tooth from the convention she's going to."

Meg stuck out her tongue. "I already have one, *and* a clock shaped like a tooth, *and* about a thousand toothbrushes," she said with a pout. "I still don't know why you can't bring me on the trip."

"Now, Meg," Mrs. Milano said. "It's settled. We'll both be way too busy. Besides, you have so much homework over the vacation, plus piano practice, and planning your next science project. Anyway, I thought you'd be so happy about Aunt Teddy coming."

"So you could eat chocolates for breakfast and stay up late watching television," Mr. Milano teased.

Mrs. Milano put her hands on her hips the way Meg always imagined she did when she'd been a teacher and had to scold the class. In fact, just like Mrs. Higgle, an unpopular teacher at Meg's school, Mrs. Milano was using her reading glasses as a pointer to scold Meg's dad. "Now,

Peter, don't be giving Meg any more crazy ideas. It's going to be hard enough getting Teddy to make sure Meg gets her homework done and gets started on her science project, and . . ."

Meg went upstairs and left her parents arguing about all the calamities that might befall their daughter once Aunt Teddy took over. Meg could hardly wait. Why, maybe she wouldn't even pick up her socks while her parents were gone! Or maybe she'd forget to do her homework one night. Something criminal like that would really teach her parents not to go off on free trips without her!

Standing over her tidy desk and looking out her bedroom window, Meg could see bright patches of colors flashing through the branches of the maple tree. She had hoped nobody would come inside with her. Unfortunately, as she often did when she was grumpy, Meg wished for the opposite thing, too. Why didn't her friends follow her inside and *beg* her to join them?

Meg looked down at her Friends 4-Ever clipboard and decided to write a letter, but not to her traitor friends who seemed to be having fun in *her* personal maple tree without her! No, she would write a letter to Aunt Teddy, that's who. She would write down all the neat things they

11

could do while Meg's parents were gone. So she began a different kind of Meg Milano list, not at all practical or sensible.

Dear Aunt Teddy,

Remember I wrote to you about the Friends 4-Ever Club I started with my friends Laura and Stevie when Molly went to Kansas? Well, it's still going — sort of — and I want you to help us think of new stuff to do, especially me. Sending this letter makes you an honorary member. I'm doing what you said — thinking of fun things we can do when you get here. Are you ready for my wish list? Here goes:

I wish you would let me watch One Family Too Many (just once so I could tell kids at school that I saw it).
I wish you would help me straighten my hair. (Yes, I still hate having curly hair!)
I wish you would wake me up for a come-

see-the-moon party like we did last time. (I loved that.)

I wish you would bring me and the Friends 4-Ever to the Megaplex and go see a movie while we see a different one. Would you believe we're the only kids on the planet our age who always have to have our parents sitting in the same theater with us?

I wish you would remind my parents that I'm practically the only eleven-year-old earthling who doesn't have pierced ears, either. (Even Molly has them!)

If you do join the circus, like Mom says, can you bring me, too?

I'm sorry you missed my birthday, but thanks for the I Spy Kit. I can't wait to find out about the other birthday surprise you mentioned on the phone.

　　　　　　Yours 'til the wind chimes,

　　　Love,
　　　　　Meg

Meg read over her letter, then added a P.S. and two other P.S.'s that took up another sheet of paper. By the time she was done, she felt better. There was something about making lists

13

on her nice cat stationery that always made her feel as if solving the world's problems was a cinch.

Meg tiptoed to the guest room across the hall and put the letter on the pillow where Aunt Teddy would be sure to find it. As she was leaving, she heard giggling coming from outside the window her mother had opened to air out the guest room. When she looked out at the tree branches, she saw the binoculars aimed right at her.

"WE KNOW YOU'RE IN THERE. COME OUT WITH YOUR HANDS OVER YOUR HEAD!" an unfamiliar voice said.

"WHO'S OUT THERE?" Meg yelled out the window.

"IT'S THE MYSTERY WOMAN," the unfamiliar voice answered.

Who *was* that? Meg tried to peek out the window without being seen. Pulling back the curtain, she saw four, not three, pairs of legs hanging from the branches.

"I SAID, WHO IS IT?" she yelled again.

"COME OUT AND SEE," the mystery voice answered.

In a flash, Meg raced downstairs and out the front door to find out who had invaded her private-for-members-only-exclusive-everyone-

14

else-keep-out-spying tree. Looking up into the branches from the ground, she recounted legs. When she got to the fourth pair, she could see they didn't belong to anyone she knew. Shana McCardle, a friend of all the girls, was the only person Meg knew who might possibly wear two sneakers that didn't match. But Shana was down in Florida visiting relatives during the spring break. So who belonged to the mismatched sneakers?

With a crash, a long-legged girl with a mass of blonde curls made a daring jump at least six feet down. When she landed smoothly on her feet, the breathless girl said to Meg, "Hi! I'm Maxine Grant, and thanks for letting me use your tree."

If Wonder Woman had jumped out of her spying tree, Meg wouldn't have been more surprised. This tall girl with gold-flecked hazel eyes and a smattering of golden freckles to match might as well have been wearing a bright red cape—that's how amazing she looked to Meg.

"My family just got here about a half hour ago. When I heard voices up in your tree, I just had to find out who they belonged to," this girl named Maxine said. "Hope you don't mind my barging in. My parents tell me I'm Queen of the Bargers."

Meg didn't know what to say and looked up the tree trunk for help from her friends who were making their way down branch by branch.

Stevie landed first with her usual crash. "Well, Meg, you got your wish."

"What's that?"

Stevie grinned and pointed to the girl. "Somebody different moved next door to you. Real different."

TO THE MAX

Maxine Grant was different all right, the way a hurricane is different from a light spring breeze, and she blew into Meg's life just when Meg needed a change of weather. From the minute Maxine jumped out of the spying tree, it seemed to Meg that Maxine had been part of their group forever.

Just two days after the Grants moved in next door, Meg automatically counted out five, not four, sets of scrap paper, pencils, erasers, and stacks of math problems the volunteers from the Children's Hospital had sent over for the Math Marathon.

"So what are you lecturing on today, Meg-o?"

Mr. Milano asked when he walked by Meg's room. He couldn't help noticing it looked more like a classroom than a bedroom.

"Oh, Dad," Meg sighed. "I told you. We have to do a thousand math problems at a nickel apiece to raise fifty dollars for the Children's Hospital. That's our Friends 4-Ever project for spring vacation."

"No wonder you've been looking so glum," Mr. Milano chuckled. "Doesn't sound nearly as much fun as running around the neighborhood solving mysteries."

"Now, Peter," Meg's mother scolded when she overheard this. "This is a wonderful way for the girls to pass the vacation. It'll give them something to do and reinforce their math skills at the same time."

"Whoopee," Mr. Milano said. He winked at Meg, who wasn't exactly jumping up and down at the idea of doing a thousand math problems over vacation, even if it was for a good cause.

A soft thud against the outside wall of her bedroom saved Meg from having to think any more about how disgustingly practical her mother was. Why, oh why, did she always approve of things like Math Marathons, and disapprove of stuff like the I Spy Kit?

18

Luckily Meg's parents didn't notice the thud of one of the tennis balls Maxine and Meg used to signal each other between their houses. Meg waved away her snoopy parents, closed the door, and flung open her window.

"Hi," Meg cried out to Maxine. "How come you're not here yet? Our meeting starts in a couple of minutes."

Maxine held up a small green bottle. "Here's why. I'll send this over on the Hotline basket."

Maxine pulled on a rope clothesline the girls had rigged up between their two bedrooms. The little basket dangling from it inched along toward Meg's bedroom. She took the bottle out of the basket and pulled out the note that was curled up inside.

HELP! I'M SHIPWRECKED. IF ANYONE READS THIS NOTE, PLEASE SEND HELP TO MY BEDROOM. I CAN'T LEAVE UNTIL I FINISH UNPACKING, PER ORDERS OF MY CAPTORS.
             DESPERATELY YOURS,

Maxine

Meg giggled and gave Maxine a big smile. The

Hotline, the little notes in the bottle — Maxine always put a fun twist on things. She'd get the Friends 4-Ever out of the rut Meg thought they were in, that was for sure.

"Hang on, Maxine, we'll come over as soon as everyone gets here," Meg called out.

Maxine wasn't in any hurry to unpack the many cardboard boxes that cluttered her room. Instead, she leaned out the window and began chatting with Meg while they waited for the others to arrive. As Maxine talked, Meg studied, once again, the way Maxine looked. She was like no other girl Meg knew. First of all, there was the hair. Meg couldn't get over how Maxine didn't even try to smooth out the tangle of blonde curls that sprang out in a hundred directions. Maxine was the only person she'd ever seen, outside the movie stars, that is, who only had *one* ear pierced — and it had three holes in it! On this sunny afternoon, all three silver studs twinkled on Maxine's right ear. Nothing about Maxine matched — not her socks, not her shoes, not even her ears!

Suddenly Meg jumped when someone inside tickled her. "Eeee!" she screamed as she pulled herself in from the window, bumping her head.

"Surprise!" Stevie shouted to an annoyed

Meg. "Hi, Maxine. Wanna see if I can broad jump from here to your room?"

"Sure, go ahead. Then I'll try," Maxine kidded back.

Laura, who was always careful about heights, didn't even like to joke about such a thing. "Don't you dare, you two." She grabbed Stevie by her belt loop. "Get back in here, Stevie."

Maxine winked across to Laura. "Thanks, Laura. Sometimes I do need someone to keep me from breaking my neck, and today you're it."

Molly, who had come into Meg's room behind Laura, wondered what all the excitement was about. "Hey, I thought we were having our meeting at four, and it's past that already," she said in mock horror. Meg was usually very particular about starting the Friends 4-Ever meetings on the dot.

"See you in a while," Meg called out before she shut her window. "My public is waiting."

Laura, Stevie, and Molly settled into their usual sitting places on the floor. Everyone waited for Meg to blow on the silver whistle she always used to start the meetings. But the whistle was nowhere to be seen.

"Hey, guys, we have to go help Maxine," Meg

began. "Her parents won't let her come over until she unpacks some more stuff."

Laura looked at Meg with a question in her big brown eyes. "I didn't know Maxine was coming to the meeting." She said this in a soft, hesitant voice so no one would think she wanted Maxine left out. After all, she liked Maxine a lot. Everybody did, but Laura wasn't quite ready to spend every minute with her, either, especially the precious minutes of Friends 4-Ever meetings.

Unlike Laura, Molly did not use a soft voice and she got straight to the point. "How can somebody come to a Friends 4-Ever meeting if she's only been a friend a couple of days? I mean, I like her and all. How could I not since she likes horseback riding *and* art? But still, usually, it's just us."

Stevie, who was good at keeping score on and off the field, nodded along with Laura and Molly. "Yeah, Meg, Molly's got a point. We haven't exactly known her *forever*. And we are the Friends 4-*Ever*, you know."

Meg's dimpled, happy face went from pink to red. Who was in charge of things like meetings and members, anyway? Hadn't she, Meg Milano, had the idea way back when to start a club of friends that would keep the girls together until Molly got back from Kansas? "Um, I didn't know we couldn't bring in new friends. We all like her, so what's the problem?"

No one could say anything to this without sounding like they were so snobbish they wouldn't let in somebody new, so the room was silent.

Then Laura remembered something that made everything okay again. "I guess it's like that time I brought Shana to the meeting, and you guys didn't want her. But then we all wound up liking her after all. Sometimes she hangs out with us and sometimes she doesn't, but it's fun when she does come."

"That's absolutely right," Meg said.

"All right, already, with all this talking about who can come and who can't," Stevie said. "If Maxine is coming, then let's go help her unpack, so we can get going on the horrible Math Marathon problems that you and Molly signed us up for. Blech!"

Molly's face grew red, and she pulled on her little horseshoe earrings the way she always did when she was trying to control her famous temper. "Stevie! I told you Meg and I could do a lot of the problems, so you won't have so many. Besides, now that Maxine is coming, I guess it'll go faster. She mentioned yesterday they were on long division and decimals at her old school, and those are worth ten cents each. She can do those, and you can stick with the easier problems."

"The girl's a triple threat, make that a quintuple threat, no doubt about it." Stevie was amazed that someone could be good at sports *and* math *and* wear three pierced earrings all at the same time.

"And don't forget ballet," Laura added softly. It was hard to admit out loud that Maxine seemed to be fabulous at *everything*.

"Well, what are we waiting for? Let's go," Meg directed the group.

Mrs. Milano looked puzzled when the girls headed out the back door toward the Grants' house. "I thought you girls would be racing through math problems by now," she said before Meg could make her escape.

"Not yet," Meg explained. "Maxine's coming to the meeting, but first we have to help her unpack."

Mrs. Milano's eyebrows shot up. "I didn't know Maxine was in your club." Before continuing, she waited for the other girls to go out and spoke to Meg privately. "Don't rush ahead with Maxine too fast, honey. Sometimes people like that can be disappointing if you try to get friendly too soon."

24

This was just too much for Meg, it really was. "People like what, Mom? I thought we were supposed to be neighborly and welcome new people and everything. You always say that. Now you're saying the opposite."

Mrs. Milano put down the carrot peeler she was holding. "Let's keep our voices down," she said in a low, serious voice. "I do want us to be neighborly, but let's take it slowly, that's all I'm saying. Maxine, plus her family, well, they've been over here constantly since they moved in. Daddy and I just think we should take a little more time to get to know each other before we're at each other's houses all the . . ."

She stopped talking and looked over Meg's head. "Oh, hello, Serena," she said, raising her voice in a chirpy way that Meg hated.

Serena Grant, Maxine's mother, had just sailed in the back door for the umpteenth time that day.

"We were thinking of ordering Chinese food and wondered if you, Peter, and Meggie here would like to join us," Mrs. Grant said.

"Can we, Mom, can we?" Meg begged without waiting for her mother to make up her own mind.

"Sorry, Meg, it's our last night for just the three of us to have dinner before we go away.

I think we have to turn you down, Serena, but thank you so much, anyway. Last night was lovely. Thanks again."

What a party pooper. Hadn't the Milanos, just the night before, enjoyed the Mexican meal the Grants had ordered in from Casa Miguel? They'd all sat on a blanket, picnic style, in the Grants' empty living room with little candles flickering all over the place and mariachi music blasting from a tape recorder, gobbling up tacos and nachos and all kinds of goodies. Meg decided her mother was just annoyed that the Grants had passed up an invitation to eat a plain old casserole at the Milanos' dining room table with no candles and no music. Her parents just didn't know how to have fun.

"Oh, come on," Mrs. Grant coaxed. "It'll be fun. We really do have a table and chairs to sit on now. It could be a bon voyage party. Why don't you ask Peter? Peter, are you in the house, Peter?" Mrs. Grant sang out.

Mrs. Milano didn't budge. "Peter's trying to meet a deadline on his medical newsletter before we leave, and the same goes for me with my newsletter for the orthodontic group, so I'm afraid we have to say no."

Mrs. Grant wasn't about to be put off by something boring like dental and medical newsletters.

"All the more reason not to cook. C'mon, Meg. I'll bet you can convince your mother."

By the look on Mrs. Milano's face and the fierce way she was scraping carrots into the garbage, Meg knew Mrs. Grant had already lost her bet. And Meg knew better than to ask. "See you later. We'll be in Maxine's room."

By the time Meg got there, any thoughts of the Math Marathon problems were pretty far away. Both Maxine and Molly were wearing horseback-riding helmets and admiring Maxine's wardrobe of riding pants and boots. Stevie, meanwhile, had lined up all Maxine's sports trophies in gymnastics, soccer, and swimming.

"Boy, you must keep the engravers busy," Stevie said with a whistle. "How many sports do you go out for, anyway?"

Maxine stopped to think. "I don't know. Lots. Since we've moved so much, my parents think sports are a good way to meet kids fast, so my sister and I have had tons of lessons."

"Luckee," Stevie answered, admiring a group shot of Maxine at some kind of fancy soccer camp. "You should try out for Select Soccer after vacation. It's the best."

"After we sign her up at Miss Humphrey's," Laura broke in when she discovered a pair of well-worn satin toe shoes in one of the boxes.

"Of course, Molly and I haven't graduated to *pointe* yet, but maybe next year."

Maxine did a graceful *pirouette* across the floor and took a deep bow, so deep, that her forehead practically touched her feet. "I saved those from the *Sleeping Beauty* I was in last fall in Indianapolis. I'm going to hang them over the bed — if anyone ever puts my bed together, that is."

Laura swung the irresistible pink toe shoes by their satin ribbons and looked around for a pushpin to put them on the wall for Maxine. "I have some toe shoes hanging over my bed, too, but they're from a real ballet star. I wish they were mine, but Miss Humphrey says I'm not ready for toe yet," Laura sighed.

Maxine put her arm around Laura and squeezed her. "It's a cinch. Tomorrow I'll show you and Molly some of the stretches you can do to get ready for *pointe*. Maybe you can surprise your teacher, and she won't make you wait a whole year."

"You don't know Miss Humphrey." Molly stroked a pair of well-worn riding boots that Maxine had unpacked. "She's real strict, and she never lets anybody jump ahead."

"She will when she sees me!" Maxine said as she spun around on one foot like a perfectly balanced top. "Ta dah! Now enough with dancing. Why don't we go to that place in town, that ice-cream place you told me about, with the *Wizard of Oz* name. What's it called?"

"The Yellow Brick Road!" the girls shouted out together.

Meg surveyed Maxine's room. It still looked more like the inside of a moving van than a bedroom. All the boxes were opened, but not a single one was completely unpacked. The few things they had taken out — Maxine's riding gear, the ballet stuff, and some of her sports equipment — lay every which way all over the room. Meg would no more have been able to sleep in a room like that than in the middle of Main Street.

"Why don't we put some of this stuff away, and then get at least one box emptied out?" Meg suggested. "And we really should do a few problems on the Math Marathon stuff at my house."

"Oh, Meg, don't be such a camp counselor," Maxine teased. With this, she tossed a soccer ball over to Stevie who was only too glad to fool around instead of doing something practical like unpacking. "We'll get stuff done after dinner while our parents are talking."

"But, but," Meg sputtered. "My mom says we

can't come over since it's our last night before my parents go on their trip. She just told your mother we can't."

"Don't worry about that," Maxine said as she fished around in her closet for two different-colored sneakers to put on. "My mom'll talk her into it, you'll see. But meanwhile that Chinese meal is hours away, and my stomach is screaming for ice cream. Aaaa! Oooo!" she screamed at the top of her lungs. "So what're you guys waiting for?" Maxine asked. "Aren't you starving already?"

Meg decided to deliver the bad news that she wasn't allowed to go out to the Yellow Brick Road so close to dinnertime. She could just see her mother screaming about ice cream, too, but not at all in the way Maxine was.

Meg shifted from one sneaker to the other. "See I don't think we can go. We were . . . uh . . . supposed to have a meeting, you know, and do the math problems for the marathon. That's the only reason I could have everybody over."

"Oh, how boring!" Maxine said. "We can sit down and do those thousand problems in one afternoon before school starts again. I told you I'm great at math, so let's not waste the rest of today. I'm going to kidnap you."

Maxine took a jump rope that was hanging off

one of the sports equipment boxes and lassoed Meg around the waist. Laura, Molly, and Stevie couldn't stop giggling at the sight of Meg Milano being bossed around instead of *doing* the bossing.

"Stevie, grab that red bandanna and blindfold Meg."

"Help, I'm being kidnapped," Meg protested between her own giggles as Maxine led her downstairs.

Mrs. Grant looked up from a box of dishes she was unpacking and joined in the fun. "Just do what she says, Meg," Maxine's mother told her. "When Maxine makes up her mind, you're done for, I'm afraid."

Maxine undid the blindfold. "I caught this rustler up in ma room," she said in a rough western-accented voice. "Now I hafta bring her ta justice in town, and I needa stagecoach to bring her in."

Mrs. Grant rolled her eyes. "Where to now, Maxine?"

"Just to a place called the Yellow Brick Road in town. Can we, Mom?" Maxine pleaded. "We're practically all unpacked and need a treat after all the work we did. Can you drop us off there?"

Mrs. Grant, who was nowhere near unpacked,

31

either, seemed to welcome an excuse to get away from the chaos. "Well, okay, girls. Hop in the car, and I'll get my keys."

Despite all the giggling, and wrestling, and fooling around, Meg knew she should run into her house and tell her mother where she was going. But when she got into the Grants' car, she saw her mother's head bent over the sink. She was probably washing vegetables, Meg knew. Then Mrs. Grant came out and started the car, and it was too late for Meg to do anything.

Besides, she was being kidnapped. If the Milanos wanted Meg back, well, they'd just have to pay ransom at the Yellow Brick Road!

ELEVEN GOING ON
TWO YEARS OLD

Meg lay back on her bed and listened to the soft tick of the tooth-shaped clock on her bedroom wall. "Only one more hour, and I'll be free," she told her cat, Marmalade, who was lying curled in a circle of sunshine at the foot of the bed.

As Meg stared up at the late afternoon shadows that waved and stretched across the ceiling like a witch's fingers, she felt good and sorry for herself. The whole world, well, *practically* the whole world, was out having fun today except for Meg, who still had fifty-seven minutes of her punishment left to go. Well, if her parents thought she had spent the afternoon in her room doing homework on a vacation day just because she was grounded, they were dead wrong. Meg's bulging backpack leaned like an unopened bag of potatoes next to her desk.

Suddenly she heard a soft thud against the house. A few seconds later, she heard it again. Startled, both she and Marmalade jumped from the bed. But unlike Marmalade, who went to hide under the desk, Meg ran to the window where Maxine was about to lob another tennis ball across to the Milanos' house.

"Did they let you out of jail yet?" Maxine called out when Meg opened the window.

Meg shook her head "No" but didn't say a word. After all, she wasn't supposed to speak to anyone for fifty-six more minutes until the warden set her free.

"Poor you," Maxine called out, pretending to sniffle in sympathy for Meg. "Here, pull the basket in. There's a note in it. I know you can't talk, but I hope your parents will let you read at least."

Meg gave Maxine a sad smile, then tugged on the Hotline rope and reeled in the basket. Inside was a piece of gum, which Meg unwrapped and chewed like a hungry prisoner, and a small note, which she unfolded and began to read.

Dear Meg,

Boo hoo, I miss you. Sorry my mom and I got you in trouble yesterday. I didn't know people in Rhode Island got grounded for eating ice cream before dinner! The worst thing was not having you come over last night. Whew, next time we'll just have bean sprouts.

I hope your parents aren't still mad at me when they come back from their trip. I'll stay out of sight until they go.

Friends 'til the ice screams,

Maxine

Meg had just bunched up Maxine's note and tossed it to Marmalade when she heard another tap, this time at her bedroom door. She pretended not to hear it and didn't say a word. Finally, the door opened, and there stood her mother.

"I know it's not six o'clock yet, but Dad just convinced me that you probably had enough. Besides Aunt Teddy should be here any second, and I would hate to have us not talking to each other."

Not talking was just what Meg continued to do.

"Now, Meg," Mrs. Milano began when she sat on the bed to get Meg's attention. "The rule about letting us know where you are is for safety reasons, that's all. It's like when you were little and we were so strict about not letting you run in the road. Some things are just plain dangerous."

Though she wouldn't turn around to face her mother, Meg tucked her gum under her tongue and finally broke her silence. "I didn't know eating ice cream before dinner was dangerous."

Meg heard her mother take a deep breath while she tried to find words that would keep them from having another blow-up. "As Dad and I told you last night, it wasn't the ice cream. It was going out for the ice cream without saying a word."

"But I told you, I thought Mrs. Grant would call you when she went to get her keys."

Mrs. Milano got up from the bed and came around to the side of Meg's bed. "Aw, Meg. Let's not go over that again. It's up to you to tell us — no, *ask* us — about whether you can go out, when you're going out, and where you're going."

Meg made herself very straight and stiff on

the bed. What were her parents going to demand next? A sign-out book by the front door? Or maybe a Secret Service bodyguard just like the President had?

"May I go to the bathroom now?" Meg asked. "It's down the hall, and I'll be back in five minutes. I promise to look both ways when I walk past the stairs in case there's traffic coming."

Mrs. Milano threw her hands up in the air, but she was smiling. "Okay, I get the message," she said with a chuckle. "Sometimes I think I'm just too old to be the mother of a ten-year-old."

"Eleven, Mom!" Meg protested. "I'm eleven now!" Why did everyone keep forgetting this vitally important fact?

Before her mother could think of anything else to lecture about, Meg escaped downstairs and collided with her father who had just come in the front door.

Without even saying hi to Meg he yelled out, "Diane? Diane? Did that sister of yours happen to call here while I was out searching the Providence train station for her?"

"Mom's upstairs," Meg said as she backed a couple of feet away from her very annoyed-looking father. "Where's Aunt Teddy? I thought you were supposed to pick her up in time for dinner."

Mr. Milano tossed his car keys and wallet down on the hall table and bellowed up the stairs again. "Diane?"

When Mrs. Milano came down, she knew right away that there was no Aunt Teddy. "Didn't the train come in?"

"The train came in."

"Teddy wasn't on it?"

"No, Teddy wasn't on it," Mr. Milano answered in a singsongy voice. "So the question is: WHERE IS SHE?"

"Did you look around the station?" Mrs. Milano asked.

"Of course I looked around the station, Diane. At least seventeen times. Then I had two cups of coffee. Then I had her paged. But your sister does not seem to be in the state of Rhode Island."

"I wonder what the reason is this time." Mrs. Milano sounded more fed up than worried.

Mr. Milano took off his jacket. "Maybe she did join the circus just like you said last week when she didn't show up for Meg's birthday. Does she know we're supposed to take a seven o'clock flight tomorrow morning?"

Meg's mother nodded in disgust. "This is just like the time she went off with some neighbors on a weekend trip without telling Mother and

Dad, and she called them from Lake Sissiminunu to ask them to send her bathing suit. That's Teddy all over."

Defending her missing aunt, Meg interrupted her parents' bickering. "Are you sure you wrote down the right train, Mom?" She didn't realize that asking for permission to set off a stick of dynamite in the living room would have been a better question to ask.

"Of course we — " Mrs. Milano sputtered at the very moment that the doorbell rang loudly and the front door burst open.

"C.O.D. delivery," a woman's voice giggled. "I'll need twenty-seven dollars. All I have are traveler's checks. My gosh, Meg, you're a giant!"

"Teddy!" Mrs. Milano cried. "Where were you, and how did you get here?"

Aunt Teddy took off the huge reflective sunglasses she was wearing, though the sun had gone down a while ago. She reached for Mr. Milano's wallet on the hall table. "Sorry, Peter. I'll pay you back. But I'd better give the taxi driver the money before the meter goes up to thirty-seven instead of twenty-seven dollars. I'll explain in a minute."

With that, Aunt Teddy raced down the front sidewalk and shoved a bunch of bills through the window of a yellow-and-red taxi. When she came back in, she whirled Meg around in circles until they were both laughing uncontrollably.

Finally letting go of a breathless, giggling Meg, Aunt Teddy looked up at the adult Milanos who were neither breathless nor giggling. "Uh-oh. I've only been here forty-six seconds, and I'm already in the doghouse. What did I do?" She pretended to hide behind Meg. "Hand me those flowers sticking out of that tote bag, will you, Meg?" her aunt whispered excitedly in her ear.

After Meg handed her the huge, fragrant bouquet of white and purple lilacs, Aunt Teddy presented them to Mrs. Milano. "Your favorites, Diane. Just like the ones that used to be in the backyard when we were growing up. Remember, in our old hideout?"

Mrs. Milano stood there holding the flowers stiffly.

While she wriggled out of her jacket, which was more like some sort of Mexican or Indian blanket, Aunt Teddy launched into her story. "See, the lilacs are why I missed the train I was supposed to be on. Someone got on with a bunch when it pulled into Boston, and when I sniffed them, I had to get them for you, Diane, I just had to. Anyway, the person with the lilacs told me there was a flower cart just at the end of the platform. But all they had were plain old daffodils, and my heart was set on those lilacs. So I sprinted upstairs where there used to be a flower seller, and lo and behold, there were the lilacs. But there was a line a mile long, so it took forever. When I finally came back, the train was gone. And so was my luggage, of course, which is probably in the checkroom in Providence by now. Maybe Peter can drive there and pick it up; otherwise Meg and I can go tomorrow. Anyway, I took the local train, which stops two towns over, and took a taxi from there. It was a fortune, but aren't the flowers just gorgeous, Diane?" Aunt Teddy buried her glowing, expectant face into the fragrant blossoms.

"And where's my present?" Mr. Milano asked, too amazed by Aunt Teddy's tale to do anything but make a feeble joke. "I was hoping for a bouquet of, of . . . forget-me-nots!"

Aunt Teddy gave Meg's dad a hug. "I do have something perfect for you, Peter, but of course it's in my luggage, which is in Providence by now. I hope so, anyway. You didn't go all the way up there, did you?"

"Naw, I've been sitting here the whole time, just reading the paper and watching the news," Mr. Milano joked, and the whole family laughed.

Aunt Teddy took Meg's hands into her own. "Let me get a good long look at this grown-up person who's going around pretending to be my niece. Why, we're almost the same height. I can't believe you're really twelve, Meg."

"She's not really twelve, Teddy, she's barely eleven," Meg's mother pointed out, spoiling the little thrill Meg got from having her aunt think she was older. "Now, let's catch up at dinner."

"*MMMMMRRRRRR, MMMMMMRRRRRR.*" Meg was aware that some kind of motor was on in her room, a small motor but one with a definite hum. When the sound got closer, Meg opened one eye and saw that the purring was coming from a very wide-awake Marmalade.

"Why are you up?" Meg groaned. Marmalade settled down on Meg's chest, practically cutting off her oxygen.

As soon as Meg spoke, the purring motor turned into a hungry, meowing cat. Meg squinted at the luminous hands of the tooth clock. The plastic molar showed that it was five-thirty in the morning.

Meg finally figured out what was going on when she saw two tall, dark figures standing in the doorway with their suitcases.

"Bon voyage time," Mrs. Milano whispered when she came over to Meg's bed. "I hate to wake you up so early, but our taxi to the airport will be here in fifteen minutes."

Meg sat up, wide awake now. Suddenly her parents' trip, which had seemed so far away, was about to begin. Maybe it was because it was so early and she was so tired, but Meg suddenly didn't want her parents to go. That was the truth. She was going to miss them, even the lectures and the endless reminders about doing homework and brushing her teeth. Meg fell back on her pillow, upset with herself for feeling homesick when she wasn't even leaving home!

"We'll miss you, honey," Mrs. Milano said with a definite catch in her voice. "I made some bran muffins last night after you went to bed, just so you'd have something homemade for breakfast for the next few days. Before I leave, I want to make sure Aunt Teddy is conscious."

"I'll come with you," Meg said.

Marmalade wove in and out of her legs when Meg got out of bed. But right away, the cat sensed it was hopeless to wait for her to give him his food. So he tried the same leg-rubbing trick on Mrs. Milano.

"Peter, feed the beast, will you, or I'm going to have white and orange cat hair all over these new black pants," Mrs. Milano said. "Meg and

I have to blast Teddy out of bed, or we'll never get going."

The door to the guest room squeaked open when Meg and her mother went in. Aunt Teddy was curled up with a teddy bear that Meg had left on the pillow the night before with a note that read: "*A Teddy for Teddy. Love, Meg.*"

"Wake up, Theodora," Mrs. Milano whispered to Aunt Teddy. There was no response.

"Wake up, Teddy," Meg's mother said in a louder voice.

"What time is it?" a sleepy Aunt Teddy croaked.

"Almost time for the airport," Mrs. Milano said.

Aunt Teddy uncurled herself, then sat up and crossed her legs into some kind of yoga position. "MMMMM-aaaaah, MMMM-aaaaah," she chanted right before she plopped back down with the stuffed bear. "I guess my yoga mantra doesn't work anymore."

Meg tugged on the blue-and-white-striped pajamas Aunt Teddy had borrowed from Meg the night before. Amazingly, they actually fit, though Aunt Teddy's slender ankles and wrists stuck out a little too far.

"Come on," Meg coaxed. "You promised me

chocolate for breakfast, remember?" she whispered, but not softly enough.

"Don't you two dare!" Mrs. Milano joked. "I didn't make those bran muffins for nothing."

"Okay, okay, okay," Aunt Teddy said. "I'm up, but the minute that taxi leaves, Meg and I are going straight back to bed and watch a couple *I Love Lucy*'s and have something yummy to eat." Aunt Teddy's eyes had finally opened and were sparkling with mischief. "Then later I thought we'd take the I Spy Kit and spy on some of the neighbors."

Mrs. Milano pretended to strangle her younger sister. "You'd better not! Now, both of you behave yourselves and come downstairs. I have a long list of things to go over."

Did she ever! Mrs. Milano had filled two whole pages of a big yellow pad with directions about everything from changing smoke alarm batteries to feeding Marmalade.

"No more than a half cup of cat food a day for Marmalade," Mrs. Milano read off her sheet as Aunt Teddy and Meg looked with glazed eyes at the job list. "Be especially careful about that!"

Meg and her aunt nodded, then leaned into each other for support as Mrs. Milano recited the contents of the open refrigerator. "This container has leftovers from last night," Mrs. Milano told Aunt Teddy, "but you might not want that until tomorrow night since we just had it last night."

Aunt Teddy turned to Meg and made funny faces while Meg tried not to giggle. Opening the vegetable crisper, Meg saw four colored plastic containers, and she knew what her mother was going to say next.

"There are cut-up green beans in the green container, carrot sticks in the orange, and — "

"And red lollipops in the red one," Aunt Teddy teased.

Mrs. Milano didn't skip a beat. "Lollipops are your department, Teddy. All I can say is make Meg brush her teeth, promise? After all, I have a reputation to keep up with the dentists I write for. And if Meg can't brush right away, as least have her rinse out with water. Plaque starts within twenty minutes of eating, you know," Mrs. Milano said. Much to her relief Meg could see that her mother was teasing Aunt Teddy to make sure she was paying attention.

"Perish the thought!" Aunt Teddy groaned. "Now, Diane, I'm sure Meg and I will do fine, so you can stop with the veggie tour. We'll find everything. You'd better get going. I think I just heard the taxi pull up." Aunt Teddy tried to pry

46

Mrs. Milano away from her notepad and the refrigerator. "Go. Have a wonderful time. Don't worry about us. Meg and I will have a great time, too."

"That's what I'm afraid of," Mrs. Milano complained, but she gave Meg and Aunt Teddy each a big hug anyway. "Now, Teddy, I wrote everything down, Meg's assignments for school, her schedule for piano practice — "

"Mom!" Meg interrupted. "I think I know my own schedule and my homework. You didn't have to write it down."

"You're right, honey, I'm sorry." Mrs. Milano turned to her sister. "Meg's more organized than I am half the time. She'll be fine. Now watch out for the new neighbors. They're very nice, but a little too nice, if you know what I mean."

Aunt Teddy cocked her head sideways. "How can somebody be too nice, Diane? That's not even possible."

Meg knew what her mother meant, but she put on a puzzled expression, too, so her mother would see she was on Aunt Teddy's side.

"Well, they seem to have different ideas about things, and I don't want Meg to get carried away. She can tell you what happened, then you'll know what I mean."

"Yes, they eat children over there, Teddy,"

47

Mr. Milano said impatiently. "Diane, we have to leave. It's too late to train Teddy now."

Meg and Aunt Teddy gave the Milanos one final hug apiece then pushed them out the door. Still that didn't stop Meg's mother from shouting out more instructions as she got into the taxi. "I left the plumber's phone number on the counter and . . ."

"And what, Diane?" Aunt Teddy asked through chattering teeth.

"There's broccoli on sale at the Grand Union!"

When the taxi door finally closed on Meg's parents, Aunt Teddy and Meg staggered into the house, chilly and tired. "And there's a leftover chocolate bar in my tote bag," Aunt Teddy said with a giggle. "Let's go back upstairs and see if *I Love Lucy* is on yet."

4

TROUBLE WITH
A CAPITAL M

Later on that morning, when the phone rang at ten-thirty, Meg, Aunt Teddy, and Marmalade were sprawled out on the guest room bed, sound asleep in front of the little television set.

"Hmmm. Is that a real phone ringing or a television phone?" Meg mumbled when the ringing didn't stop.

"Television phone," Aunt Teddy said sleepily. She felt around the bed for the remote control. "Here, I'll turn it off."

The television went off, but the ringing didn't. Finally Meg got up and ran to her parents' room to answer the phone and put an end to the noise.

"Meg, it's Laura. How come you didn't call

anybody to tell us what we're doing today?" Meg heard her friend say.

"Hey, what time is it, anyway?" Meg asked Laura, not quite sure even what day it was.

"Ten-thirty," Laura told Meg. "Remember, you said you'd call everybody or leave notes in our mail spots to let us know what we were going to do today? What have you been doing all morning?" Laura was puzzled. It wasn't often that Meg, the Super Planner, wasn't ready first thing in the morning with a day's worth of activities for the Friends 4-Ever.

"What have I been doing?" Meg repeated. She tried to think, then slapped her cheeks to wake herself up. "Hmm. Let's see. Well, my parents left already and got me and my aunt up in the middle of the night practically. Then Aunt Teddy and I had breakfast in bed and watched an *I Love Lucy* show and . . . well, that's the last thing I remember until the phone rang. I guess we fell back to sleep."

Laura giggled at the other end. "Boy, you sure can tell your parents are gone. Usually, you're ready with our orders by nine o'clock, and *we're* the slugabeds. Hey, how's your aunt Teddy anyway? I can't wait to see her."

Meg lay back on her parents' perfectly smooth bed. Even though they'd left in a rush just a few

50

hours before, everything looked like a hotel room that had never been used.

"Aunt Teddy's great," Meg told Laura. "It's like having a big sister. We stayed up half the night planning neat stuff to do while she's here. First of all, she said you guys can come over anytime, so spread the word. She's dying to see everyone. What else? Oh, yeah, she's taking me to the mall in Providence for a belated birthday present. She keeps calling it Makeover Day, and I can get my hair cut at Sassy Scissors."

Meg heard Laura suck in her breath. "I thought you were never getting your hair cut again, Meg! You prooomised," Laura wailed. "Didn't you say it acts straighter when it's sort of long?"

As Laura tried to talk Meg out of her Sassy Scissors visit, Meg pulled on a long strand of hair and let it go. As usual, it boinged right back to her head just like a tight spring. "Maybe if I go to a haircut place like Sassy Scissors, they'll know how to make my hair do what I want it to do, not what *it* wants to do."

Laura giggled. "You make your hair sound like it's a real person, separate from you."

"I only wish," Meg groaned.

"Well, just don't come back looking like Erica Soames and Suzi Taylor, the Know-It-Alls. You know how they're always bragging about going to Sassy Scissors for those haircuts they have. Hey, can you hang on a second, Meg? Somebody's at the front door."

Meg rolled over on her stomach and put her head down on a pillow while she waited for Laura to come back to the phone. She was still on her stomach when she felt someone tickle the soles of her feet. "Who're you talking to? Your phone's been busy for ages," Meg heard Stevie ask as she held onto her bare foot and wouldn't let go. When Meg looked up, Stevie, Molly, and Maxine were all standing in her parents' bedroom and smiling like a litter of Cheshire cats.

Meg covered the mouthpiece of the phone and whispered to the girls, "I'm talking to Laura."

"You are?" Laura said, but the voice was coming from the bedroom, not the phone. "What am I saying?"

All the girls roared at Laura's practical joke, which totally surprised Meg, something it wasn't always easy to do.

Meg threw a pencil across the room, but Laura ducked just in time. "You stinker! I've been hanging on the phone all this time waiting for you to come back."

"Yup," Laura said with a grin. "Now I'm planning to tickle you silly unless you get dressed. Your aunt Teddy's taking us to town, and she said all lazybones have to report for duty in five minutes."

Meg made it in two minutes. When she got downstairs her friends were gathered around Aunt Teddy like chattering squirrels. Aunt Teddy, whose luggage was still in Providence, had thrown one of Mrs. Milano's denim vests over Meg's pajama top and put on a borrowed pair of jeans. The whole outfit looked great, especially with the pair of wooden giraffe earrings that she'd bought in Africa a few years before when she was in the Peace Corps. Meg had the same earrings, but of course she wouldn't be able to wear them for several centuries until her parents let her pierce her ears.

"Well, Meg, I just met Maxine for the first time, and we discovered we both have the same astrological sign, Aquarius. Now you won't have to wait for your wild and crazy aunt to do nutty things; you've got a wild and crazy friend right next door. Maxine and I, with these other three guys, have been cooking up some incredible plans for the vacation."

"I thought you were only going to be here two weeks, Aunt Teddy, not two months," Meg kidded when she saw the long Things-to-Do list scrawled out in bright purple marker on a piece of her cat stationery.

THINGS TO DO

Try out I Spy Kit.
Play some soccer.
Everybody try on one outrageous outfit at
Steinbach's.
Stop at parrot machine in shoe store.
Each person take $2.00 and buy silliest thing
in Camden for someone else.
Visit pet store and think of names for all the
pets in the window.
Sign up Maxine at Miss Humphrey's Dance
Studio.
Have ice cream at Yellow Brick Road.

"Uh-oh, Aunt Teddy," Meg warned. "You can get put in jail for that last item on your list."

"Oh, no! I'm worried now," Aunt Teddy joked. "Now let's get going on Item Number

Two, playing a little soccer at the middle school field. Lead the way."

"What about the Math Marathon problems?" Molly reminded everyone. "You didn't put those on the list."

Maxine pinched her nose and yelled, "Boo hiss," while Stevie stomped her feet in protest.

"We have to get started on them." Molly turned to Meg for help, but it was too late. Maxine had already grabbed Meg and dragged her to the front hall closet for her jacket so they could get going. From the sound of Meg's giggling protests, math problems weren't exactly at the top of Meg's Things-to-Do list, either.

While everyone put on their jackets, Stevie grabbed a green-and-black soccer ball from the hall closet along with the I Spy Kit.

"Oh, goody," Aunt Teddy said. "Here, let me try the periscope. You girls go out and do something, and I'll try to watch you with this from inside the house."

The girls raced out to the curb, and Maxine and Meg did headstands on the lawn.

Aunt Teddy ran out with the periscope. "I saw you doing headstands!" she called out.

Maxine, Stevie, Molly, and Laura ran down Doubletree Court with the periscope and pointed it out from behind various trees, but there was no one out to spy on at this hour. The girls got so far ahead they were out of sight of Meg and her aunt who walked along more slowly so they could talk to each other.

"I hope the I Spy Kit didn't cause too much trouble," Aunt Teddy told Meg in a more serious voice than usual. "You know me. I love practical jokes, and I love impractical ones even better. I still like to tease your mom once in a while. She was always the serious one."

"Yeah, tell me about it," Meg grumbled.

Aunt Teddy took Meg's hand. "Why don't you tell *me* about it. Things a little tense lately between you two?"

Meg kicked at pebbles with her sneaker. "Sort of, " she mumbled. "It's just that Mom and Dad never let me do *anything*. *They're* the ones who are always spying on *me*."

"Spying?" Aunt Teddy asked.

"Well, watching over me all the time. I guess it's because I'm an only child. They're just always there looking at my homework book, noticing if my toothbrush was used, or if my clothes don't go together."

Now Aunt Teddy put an arm around Meg, and they walked shoulder to shoulder like that for the rest of the block. "Well, your mom was the oldest of the five of us. Since your grandmother was sick a lot, your mother was the one who had to make sure we brushed our teeth and that we didn't go to school dressed like ragamuffins. I guess she still can't stop being the big sister, even to me," Aunt Teddy said in a sad way. "She'll always think of the rest of us as little kids, especially me."

Meg suddenly gave her wonderful, super aunt a huge hug. "That's what makes you fun, Aunt Teddy," Meg said.

Feeling better now, Aunt Teddy and Meg skipped along to catch up to everyone. When they turned the corner onto Crispin Landing Road, they expected to see the girls strolling ahead. Instead, Stevie, Laura, and Molly were standing in front of an old man who seemed to be scolding them. Off to the side was Maxine, who was pointing the periscope at the old man from behind a tree.

"Uh-oh, that's Mr. Melham," Meg said. "He hates kids. I wonder if someone stepped on his lawn by mistake." She slowed down in the hopes that Mr. Melham would go back into his house before she and her aunt reached his yard.

"Are you looking after these kids?" Mr. Melham screamed at Aunt Teddy when she got a little closer. The old man shook his finger at Maxine. "That one behind me there ran into my backyard without permission and pointed that periscope thing through my kitchen window. Do you know that's illegal? And, while they were at it, these kids trampled on my flower beds, too. I have a good mind to call Chief Weaver and tell him these kids were trespassing on my property, not to mention whatever criminal thing they're doing with that device."

Except for Maxine, the girls stood shamefaced, shifting from foot to foot and looking as if they wanted to sink into the ground. They knew how much time Mr. Melham spent caring for his garden. Even worse, they knew Mr. Melham's wife had just gotten out of the hospital.

Meg felt horrible, yet at the same time it was hard to look serious while Maxine kept pointing the periscope at Mr. Melham. While Aunt Teddy signaled Maxine to put it away, Meg and the other girls tried to keep straight faces. Meg just wanted to escape so she could get rid of the tangle of feelings she had. Her heart was pounding, she felt horrible for Mr. Melham, yet she didn't know how long she could keep from laughing out loud.

When Maxine finally stopped fooling around behind Mr. Melham, Laura was the first one to pull herself together and apologize. "I'm sorry, Mr. Melham," Laura said, then Stevie and Molly mumbled something that sounded like an apology, too.

Aunt Teddy thrust out her hand to Mr. Melham, who ignored it. "I'm Theodora Biddle, Diane Milano's sister, and I'm very sorry we disturbed you, sir. I know the girls didn't mean to run on your lawn. They've been doing some bird-watching and got carried away. I'll make sure they confine their observations to trees and bushes from now on."

This didn't soften Mr. Melham a bit. "No, *I'll* make sure of that if I see them anywhere near here." With that, Mr. Melham walked back to his house slowly and tiredly.

Stevie kicked at the curb in embarrassment. "I feel horrible."

"So do I," Molly and Laura joined in.

Maxine was the least upset of all. "Oh, he could have taken it as a joke."

Turning to Maxine, Aunt Teddy said, "You know what? Let me take that thing, Maxine. We'll just use it around our own house with each other." Aunt Teddy shoved the periscope and the binoculars deep into her tote bag. "Now maybe after Mr. Melham cools down, you girls can go over there and offer to do some kind of little jobs for him — maybe we can pick up some groceries for him when we go into town tomorrow or do some yard work — something like that."

"Hey, what if we made the Melhams a fantastic dinner?" Maxine cried. "A big lasagna with lots of melted cheese! I'll get my mom and my big sister to help me do that tonight, and you guys can get the other fixings. We'll make it fun."

What an incredible idea! Meg felt as if a huge weight had lifted off her. They'd make it up to Mr. Melham.

Of course they would.

OUT OF CONTROL

Laura showed up at Meg's the next day carrying a small white pastry box. Following right behind was Stevie, waving around a long, skinny loaf of Italian bread.

"En garde," she said to Molly who also arrived with a long loaf of bread.

While the girls pretended to sword fight with their loaves, Meg tossed some of her mother's raw vegetables into a bowl of lettuce. "Should I pour this dressing over the salad now, or just give the Melhams the bottle so they can put it in the salad when they have our dinner?"

Aunt Teddy was too busy folding red, green, and white paper napkins from the Milanos'

61

Christmas box to answer Meg right away. "I guess these will do. They're the same color as the Italian flag. Here, Meg, give me the bottle of dressing. I'll put it in the picnic basket with Laura's pastries and those loaves of Italian bread, that is, if there's anything left after Stevie and Molly stop swatting them around. I'll leave room for Maxine's lasagna when she gets here. Now where's that note you wrote, Meg?"

Meg pulled out the note and read it out loud to hear how it sounded:

"To Mr. and Mrs. Melham:
We're sorry we made you glum.
We also made you dinner,
So Friends 4-Ever will be a winner.
Sorry we looked in,
We won't do that again.
About us, don't you worry,
We're very, very sorry.

Yours 'til the eye lashes,
FRIENDS 4-EVER"

Stevie's jaw dropped, and she put her hands around her throat. "Sorry and worry? Oh, gag. They don't even rhyme, Meg."

Meg handed Stevie a pencil and a pad of paper. "Okay, smarty-pants, you try."

Of course, Stevie wanted nothing to do with writing a poem.

"Sorree," Stevie said. "Worree. Yeah, I guess they do rhyme after all. Now can we go?"

"I second that!" Aunt Teddy said now that everything was ready. "Run over to Maxine's and tell her to catch up with us, Meg. We'll wait for you in front of the Melhams."

Meg cut through the backyard but didn't get very far before Maxine called down from her bedroom. "Be there in a sec. Meet me out front."

"All set," Maxine said when she finally came out to meet Meg.

Meg blinked. "Boy, I should've worn my sunglasses," she joked when she saw Maxine's wild jungle-print shoulder bag slung over a paint-splatter-printed pair of overalls. She still couldn't get over the way Maxine put together all kinds of crazy prints and colors, and it always looked fantastic. Meg's blue jeans topped off by a red sweatshirt seemed *so* boring. "Is the lasagna in your shoulder bag?"

Maxine looked completely puzzled. "A lasagna in my shoulder bag? Why would I have a lasagna in my shoulder bag?"

Meg looked at Maxine to see if she was kidding. Maybe the lasagna was still in the refrigerator, and Maxine had forgotten to get it out. "You know, the dinner we're bringing to the Melhams for making him so upset yesterday?"

Now Maxine looked even more puzzled. Not one bit of recognition flickered in her golden eyes. Meg had the feeling that she was speaking Chinese. "Remember? Aunt Teddy said we should do something for the Melhams yesterday, then you said you'd make them a lasagna, and we'd bring the rest of the stuff? Well, we have the rest of the stuff. Now all we need is your lasagna."

Maxine smacked her forehead. "Oh, that! I didn't think we were doing that right away. There's still loads of time. You mean you guys are actually bringing over the food stuff today?" When she noticed Meg's disappointed face, Maxine smacked her forehead again. "Uh-oh. Sorreee. I totally forgot. Can't we do it another day?"

"Not really," Meg answered. She looked down the street where Aunt Teddy and the girls were carrying the picnic basket between them. She just wanted to get the whole Mr. Melham mess over with, and the only thing preventing that was Maxine's missing lasagna. "Wait here," Meg finally said to Maxine. "I have to go back to my house."

Inside the kitchen, Meg opened the freezer door to the refrigerator. "Where is it? Oh, there it is," she said to herself when she spied a large, covered plastic bowl. It was the beef stew Mrs. Milano had prepared and frozen ahead for Aunt Teddy and Meg. "It's not Italian, but it'll have to do."

Meg found a plastic bag in a cupboard and stuck the big bowl in there. She didn't want anyone to ask why a flat lasagna was in a tall, round bowl.

"What's that?" Maxine asked when Meg came out with the bag.

"Dinner for the Melhams. Maybe they won't notice this is beef stew and not lasagna," Meg said in a serious voice, but Maxine thought this was a scream.

"Not notice? How could they not notice?" Maxine said, laughing, and Meg couldn't help laughing, too.

"Listen, I *am* sorry, Meg," Maxine said when she finally stopped laughing. "What with moving in and all, I totally forgot about Mr. Whats-his-name. Hey, how about if I pick up some pastries at that Italian bakery next to the Yellow Brick Road? Would that help?"

Meg held the cold wrapped package next to her. "Laura got them already. It's okay. Let's just not mention it to anybody, all right?"

"*O sole mio*," the other girls sang out in operatic voices when Meg and Maxine finally joined them.

"I hope he doesn't yell at us again," Laura said. She looked as if she'd rather deliver dinner to a starving tiger than to Mr. Melham.

"I'll go up first," Meg said firmly. "After all, it was my I Spy Kit that got us into trouble."

She rang the bell several times before Mr. Melham opened the door.

"What do you want?" he asked suspiciously when he saw everyone gathered on his doorstep.

Meg grabbed the picnic basket off the porch and set it down inside the front door. "We made you and Mrs. Melham dinner. To apologize for yesterday."

Aunt Teddy lifted her hand like a choral conductor, and the girls all sang out at the same time: "We're sorry."

Mr. Melham looked flustered at first, but then a slow smile spread over his face. "Why, why, that's quite all right. No problem at all. Sorry I got so mad. You see, it's my wife. She's been under the weather and a little touchy, you know. But she's fine now. I explained you girls were just bird-watching.''

When Meg heard that, she got a pang about the beef stew switch.

"It's a whole Italian dinner," Aunt Teddy said, making Meg cringe again and Maxine step on her foot. "The girls put it all together themselves. It was Maxine's idea here. I hope you enjoy it. *Buon appetito*," Aunt Teddy said.

After saying their good-byes to Mr. Melham, the girls felt better. Even Meg stopped wondering what the Melhams would think when their Italian meal turned out to be beef stew. It was sort of funny, when she thought about it, and she and Maxine grinned all the way to town over their little secret.

"Well, which store should we hit first?" Aunt Teddy asked when they reached the corner of Main Street and Warburton Avenue.

"Pets 'R Us!" Molly cried. "That's where my dog, Riggs, came from. They always have cute puppies in the window."

"You'll love Pets 'R Us," Meg told Aunt Teddy and Maxine. "We buy all our supplies for Marmalade there, including his diet cat food. Ooooo, look," Meg crooned when she saw several new puppies and kittens sleeping or scampering right in the window. "I wish my parents would let me get a dog."

"How about that one?" Aunt Teddy pointed to a German shepherd puppy with huge paws. "Can you imagine the fit your mother would have if we brought him home?"

"Could we, could we?" Meg pleaded.

"Sorry, kiddo, I don't want to be disowned by your family," Aunt Teddy said with a laugh.

"Boo-hoo," Meg grumbled. "Well, at least we can look."

Mr. Gleason, the owner, was sprinkling fish food into one of the aquariums when the girls came in. "Hey, it's the Friends 4-Ever gang. You girls plowed through the Math Marathon problems I sponsored yet? I know you'll raise lots of money for the Children's Hospital."

Oh, why did Mr. Gleason have to bring *that* up? Meg tried to change the subject fast. "This is my mom's sister, Aunt Teddy, and this is Maxine Grant," Meg said. "The Grants don't have any pets yet, but maybe we can change that."

"Well, browse all you want, girls. You kids are always welcome here," Mr. Gleason said with a smile before he went back to his work.

Maxine followed Meg down the dog-and-cat-toy aisle while the others stayed to watch Mr. Gleason feed the fish.

"Fetch, Meg," Maxine yelled out.

When Meg spun around, Maxine was about to toss her a huge rawhide bone. The bone was in the air before Meg had a chance to protest. Meg reached up, but the bone crash-landed into a stack of dog treat boxes that tumbled into the aisle.

"Come on, Maxine," Meg whispered. "Let's pick these up before Mr. Gleason catches us."

"He won't catch me. I'll be talking to the parrots," Maxine said before running to the back of the store. "Polly wanna cracker?" she said over and over while Meg tried to reshelve the scattered boxes.

"Bump into something, Meg?" Mr. Gleason said when he came over to check on the noise.

"Yeah, sorry, Mr. Gleason. I, uh, lost my balance, and these, uh . . . boxes fell down. I was just trying to put them back."

"EEEEEEEK! RAAAAAAWCK!"

Mr. Gleason dropped the boxes he was stacking and ran to the bird cage area, which was in a small glassed-in room at the back of his store.

"What're you doing back here?" he yelled. Maxine was desperately trying to catch a pair of frantic parakeets who were loose in the little room. "No, don't open the door!" he yelled to her.

69

But it was too late. Maxine ran from the room, and flying right behind her was a bright blue parakeet that zoomed around the store just inches above everyone's head. By this time, Aunt Teddy and all the girls were trying to catch the parakeet whenever it stopped to rest on one of the shelves. But the second anyone got too close, it zoomed off again.

"Everybody step back," Mr. Gleason ordered, though he was looking directly at Maxine. He raised a butterfly net and bagged the poor squawking bird.

The girls looked on as Mr. Gleason gently untangled the bird in his hands and returned it to its cage. Then he took the net and chased the second parakeet which, thank goodness, was still in the cramped bird room where it would be easier to catch.

The girls couldn't help laughing, they really couldn't. Giant Mr. Gleason looked like a cartoon character as he chased the tiny bird around the tiny room with the butterfly net. Each time he was about to land the bird, it would fly to another ledge or corner.

"Please, girls, don't laugh," Aunt Teddy whispered. But even she had to look away from Mr. Gleason to keep from laughing.

"Maxine, you have to go outside," Aunt

Teddy ordered. "This isn't funny. When you calm down, come back in and tell the owner just why it is you decided to release those two birds."

"I . . . " Maxine started laughing uncontrollably again. "Never mind," she added, running out of the store before she got scolded again.

Mr. Gleason's face was shining with sweat when he finally came out of the bird room. "Well, I guess I've had my exercise for the day." He turned to the girls with a tired, disappointed look. "Now, I thought you girls knew the bird room was off-limits to customers unless I go in there, too. Too many drafts when the door opens and shuts. As for opening the cages, I'm sorry your new friend didn't think a little more about that. The birds need warmth, and if one of 'em got out on a cool day, well."

" 'Bye, 'bye, birdie!" everyone heard Maxine say next when she came up to Mr. Gleason. Noticing everyone's frazzled faces, she quickly changed her own mischievious expression to match theirs. She put out her hand to Mr. Gleason. "I'm sorry. Those two parakeets were just so pretty and velvety looking. I just wanted to see what one of them felt like. If you could put my name on the cage, I'll come back with my parents and buy both of them, okay?"

Mr. Gleason melted. Who wouldn't? Now

Maxine looked so sorry about what had happened and so worried about what she'd done to the birds, everyone immediately forgot how she'd endangered them by being so careless.

"That's fine," Mr. Gleason said. Now he seemed a little embarrassed about the whole thing. "Here, I'll put 'Sold' on that cage, so no one can buy them until you come back with your family. Take a business card on the way out. Then have your folks call and let me know a good time to pick up the birds. How's that?"

"Great!" Maxine said, but she walked right by the business cards without taking one. "See you soon. I promise."

MAXED OUT

Though the girls were exhausted from their long day in town, Maxine had kept them up until nearly four o'clock in the morning during the sleepover she insisted on having at her house. Except for Maxine, none of the other girls slept too well on the wooden floor of the Grants' nearly empty den. And the fire in the fireplace that Maxine kept calling a "camp fire" just made it harder to sleep.

Sometime during the long night, Meg looked over at Laura's sleeping bag and saw her big brown eyes shining in the dying light of the fireplace embers.

"You still awake?" Meg whispered.

Laura moaned. "I feel sort of sick from that pepperoni pizza. I should have known better than to eat anything Maxine ordered. I can't believe she had the pizza place hide anchovies under the cheese! Oh, my aching stomach!"

Meg, who hated fish, especially sneaky little salty ones like anchovies, had thought Maxine's practical joke a little bit mean earlier in the evening. Still hadn't they all laughed their heads off when they tried eating around the awful gray fish that were hidden all over the pizza?

"Why're *you* awake?" Laura whispered back.

"I wanted to move my sleeping bag back from the fire. I keep hearing the logs pop and crackle, and I'm afraid one of the sparks will jump out and set my sleeping bag on fire."

"Oh, no! Now why did you have to go and say that?" Molly complained from inside her sleeping bag. "Now I won't get any sleep, either."

"Same here," a groggy Stevie joined in. "My stomach is screaming for mercy."

Meg shifted her bag up a few inches back from the fireplace again and tried to fall asleep. But now the steady rise and fall of Maxine's snoring kept her awake.

Stevie leaned over Maxine and pinched her nose for a second, but even this didn't stop the foghorn. "I can't believe she kept us up half the night making weird stuff to eat, and now she's the only one asleep. If I weren't so tired, I'd pour a glass of water over her head."

But the girls were too tired to encourage Stevie's revenge and did their best to get back to sleep.

"So how late did you stay up?" Aunt Teddy asked the girls when they sat in the Milanos' kitchen the next morning staring at their pancakes instead of eating them.

"Oh, we heard the grandfather clock in Maxine's hallway at eleven," Meg said truthfully. "After that I don't quite remember," she added, not quite so truthfully.

"I thought you girls would gobble up these chocolate-chip pancakes," Aunt Teddy said. "I tried to follow the same recipe they use at the Pancake House where I used to bring Meg when she was little."

Meg attempted to sit up a little straighter in her chair but felt herself slump right down again. "They're good, Aunt Teddy," she said, pushing around pieces of pancake without eating them. "It's just we sort of ate a lot last night."

"Yeah, a lot of anchovies!" Stevie said, unable to even look at her plate anymore.

Maxine snickered, then speared two huge

75

pieces of pancake with her fork and ate them both. "You gotta admit, it was pretty funny when you guys bit into your pieces and tasted the little fishies," she joked. "Besides, I love anchovies," she added, taking another forkful of pancakes. "And pancakes! Can I have seconds?"

A groan went around the kitchen table.

Stevie raised her head a few inches from where she was half dozing on the table. "Does anybody have a piece of paper? Please write this down: 'I, Stephanie Louise Ames, will never eat another anchovy pizza again.' "

"Put down my name, too," Meg groaned, "and add a P.S., 'I, Margaret Ellen Milano, will never stay up until three-thirty in the morning again.' "

"Three-thirty!" Aunt Teddy screamed. "I thought you said eleven o'clock."

Meg was too tired to grin, but she did manage to say, "I said I heard the clock ring at eleven. I just forgot to mention I heard it at twelve, then one, then two, then three."

Aunt Teddy pretended to looked shocked. "If your mother . . . Oh, there's the phone. I bet she has ESP and heard this whole conversation all the way to Canada."

Meg dragged her bare feet across the kitchen

floor, leaned against the wall, and picked up the phone without saying anything.

"Hello? Hello?" Meg heard her mother say at the other end. "Anybody there? Maybe I have a bad connection."

"No, I'm here, Mom," Meg finally said in a croaky voice.

"Oh, dear. Are you sick? This is the second phone call when you've sounded awful. You must be coming down with something."

Meg slid down the wall to a sitting position on the floor. How her mother could figure out how Meg felt hundreds of miles away was amazing, but she could.

"I'm not sick," Meg said in what she hoped sounded like a healthy wide-awake voice. "I just finished breakfast."

"Those bran muffins I made must be gone by now," Mrs. Milano said. "What was on Aunt Teddy's menu today?"

"Pancakes," Meg answered, hardly able to say the word without feeling queasy.

"Oh, good," Mrs. Milano chirped. "Those are always a treat. I hope she found that whole-wheat pancake mix I left in the cereal cabinet. I put a little oat bran in it to make them healthier."

"Mmm." Meg hoped her mother didn't have

X-ray vision that worked over telephone wires. If she did, she would have seen an empty bag of chocolate chips lying right by the pancake bowl.

"So what have you and Aunt Teddy been up to?" Mrs. Milano wanted to know. "Since yesterday, I mean, when I called you?"

"Oh, just hanging around, pretty much," Meg answered, deciding to skip any mention of the sleepover at Maxine's. "Aunt Teddy's bringing all of us to the Providence mall today for a birthday surprise."

Now it was Meg's turn to wonder whether there was a bad phone connection. "Mom, are you still there?"

"Uh, yes, I'm still here," Mrs. Milano answered. "I hope you've left a little time for homework and piano and planning your science project. Sounds as if you've been out every day since we left. The vacation will be over before you know it, and you don't want to save everything for the last minute."

Well, one thing Meg didn't need was her mother up in Canada lecturing her down in Rhode Island! "Mom, I'll get everything done. I always do. Is Dad there?"

Mrs. Milano spoke in a quieter voice now. "No, he's attending a conference on chicken pox.

78

Listen, honey, I'm sorry I nagged about the homework. Of course I know you'll get all your work done," her mother said, trying to make sure they didn't hang up on a bad note. "I miss you."

"Miss you, too," Meg said, though she didn't miss the lectures like the one her mother had just given her over the phone.

"I guess I don't need to talk to Aunt Teddy since we talked yesterday," her mother went on. "But do tell her to be careful about Marmalade's food again. Dr. Grano scolded me last time about his weight. Just a half a cup a day of the cat kibble, okay?

Meg groaned. Did her mother have to run Marmalade's life long distance, too? "We know, we know, Mom," Meg said. " 'Bye."

"Okay, everybody dressed and ready for Providence in fifteen minutes. I'll meet you down here after I do a few things," Aunt Teddy told everyone after Meg hung up the phone. "What's the matter, Meg? You didn't get any more assignments from your parents, did you?" her aunt joked. "Why we've barely made a dent in that job list they already gave us."

"Nope," Meg laughed. "We haven't done laundry or gone grocery shopping or sorted out the mail. . . . "

Maxine picked up Mrs. Milano's job list and began reciting a Maxine Grant Things-We've-Done list: "But we have played four games of crazy eights, eaten two pizzas, watched two and a half movies, and taken one midnight moon-watching walk, complete with skunk! Before you get to any of those real jobs on your mom's list, I'm outta here," Maxine told everyone as she breezed out the door.

"The girl never stops," Stevie muttered.

"Doesn't she know that sometimes a person likes to sit around once in a while?" Molly added. "I need a vacation from this vacation."

Laura, too, had an opinion now that both Maxine and Aunt Teddy weren't right there. "I didn't want to be a party pooper while Maxine was here, Meg, but I know I can't go to Providence with you and your aunt. I have to go to the dentist today."

"Can't you go another day?" Meg protested. "Today's my Makeover Day, and I won't be able to go through with it without you there, Laura. What's more important, your teeth or me?"

"I'm sorry, Meg," Laura said.

"Today's the last day to sign up for Select Soccer tryouts and get measured for uniforms," Stevie said. "Maxine promised she'd come, but then she decided to go to Providence with you and your aunt. I told her how strict the officials are, but she says once they see how she plays it won't matter if she doesn't show up today." Stevie shrugged her shoulders and looked a little disappointed.

"Are you going to desert me, too, Molly?" Meg asked. "You don't look too gung ho about going to Providence."

"I'm not," Molly said. "I have to catch up on homework and get started on my science project."

"Well, we hardly ever get a chance to do all this fun stuff," Meg argued. "In just a few days we'll be back to school and the same old things."

Molly finally looked up at Meg. "Speaking of that, we still haven't started work on the Math Marathon."

Meg put her hands on her hips in disgust. "That's all you guys think about! Maxine said we can whiz through that, no problem."

Surprisingly it was Stevie who spoke up next. "Yeah, yeah, yeah — just like she said she'd come with me to Select Soccer tryouts."

"And teach us exercises so we could get ready for *pointe* in ballet," Laura said miserably. "Yesterday she said she's not even going to take ballet at Miss Humphrey's. She wants to take some kind of rock dancing at Dance Craze instead and

81

thinks we all ought to do that. Molly and I love ballet. Maxine keeps promising to do stuff. Then she forgets all about it and goes on to something else."

"Deserters!" Aunt Teddy said when she came into the kitchen and saw the other girls duck out. "Well, you'll be sorry when you find out what a good time we had, right, Meg?"

"Right!" Meg answered. If they didn't want to have a ball with her, Aunt Teddy, and Maxine, well, too bad for them!

7

MEG'S MAKEOVER DAY

The glass elevator glided skyward, and Meg felt the thrill she always got when she visited the huge mall in Providence, something she didn't get to do very often. She loved the crowds, the lights, the endless choices of stores and eating places. Maxine and Aunt Teddy were full of plans for Meg's Makeover Day, and the long ride had helped her forget her disappointment that the others hadn't come along.

"Where to first?" she asked her aunt.

Winking at Maxine, Aunt Teddy said, "Never mind. Just follow us and don't ask any questions."

When the elevator doors slid open, Maxine

83

ran out so fast she nearly knocked over a woman pushing a baby stroller into the elevator.

"Whoops!" Maxine cried, but she left Meg and her aunt to apologize to the annoyed mother.

"It's okay, it's okay," the woman crooned to her baby who had awakened when Maxine jostled the stroller.

"I'd better put Maxine on a leash," Aunt Teddy said. "She gets a little too carried away, even for an Aquarian like me. Maxine! Maxine!" she called ahead. "Slow down!"

Maxine skidded to a stop just inches in front of a booth selling delicate crystal jewelry and figurines. "Watch it, miss," the manager of the booth said, but Maxine paid no attention to him.

Instead she held up a pair of crystal unicorns to her ears and showed them to Aunt Teddy and Meg. "Look at these. Aren't they great?"

"Those are glass ornaments, not jewelry," the owner of the booth told Maxine. "See the sign? It says 'PLEASE ASK FOR HELP.'"

"Help!" Maxine said with a laugh, then tossed the fragile ornaments back on the counter. Again she raced through the mall like a rocket and only stopped when she saw a pet store window full of animals for sale.

"Uh-oh," Aunt Teddy said. "We can't let her go in there after what happened at Pets 'R Us.

C'mon, Meg. Let's get her away from that window before she lets all the animals out of their cages."

Unlike Aunt Teddy who was half joking, Meg felt a little thump in her heart. She knew Maxine hadn't even asked her parents about the birds she'd promised Mr. Gleason she was going to buy. In fact, she'd hung up on him when he called about picking up the birds. Meg kept telling herself that maybe Maxine just needed more time to soften up her parents, since they were still so busy unpacking.

"Pet stores are off-limits to certain people," Aunt Teddy scolded when she caught up with Maxine. "I'm sure two birds are all your family can handle right now, what with your moving into a new house."

"Oh, those," Maxine answered, and that was the end of her thoughts about the parakeets. "C'mon, Meg. Close your eyes and come with me."

Meg squeezed her eyes shut while Maxine and Aunt Teddy guided her a few steps down the mall arcade. Then they spun her around and told her to open her eyes. When she did, she was standing in front of a store she visited every time she came to the mall.

"The Earring Fun Factory!" she cried. "Why

did you bring me here? All they sell are pierced earrings. You know I can't get any until I'm thirty-two years old, or did my mom say forty-two? She keeps making it older and older."

Aunt Teddy grinned, and so did Maxine. What was going on?

"Well, happy thirty-two years old!" Aunt Teddy said. "Now go inside. This is my present to you, besides the I Spy Kit. Well, maybe this time your mom won't get so hysterical."

Meg's heart was pounding. What made her aunt think her mother wouldn't get hysterical about her getting her ears pierced?

Aunt Teddy cupped Meg's chin with her hand. "Hey, don't look so worried. I've been secretly wearing your mom down for months. Honest. Then yesterday she finally said: 'Well, let me think about it.' You're half a Biddle, Meg," Aunt Teddy went on. "So you know that's the Biddle way of saying yes to things they don't want to say yes to. It was always a big joke between Diane and the rest of us. So we're home free!"

Meg wasn't quite so sure of that. Unless some miraculous change had come over her mother in Canada, Meg was pretty certain her mother would need more time to think — like maybe another twenty years. Even if Aunt Teddy were right, Meg wasn't at all sure she herself was ready to have someone stick holes in her ears. In fact, her stomach was doing backflips at the very thought of it.

"No buts," Maxine insisted. "Come on. It doesn't really hurt. Besides, they put some kind of stuff on your ear to make it numb. Before you can blink, it's over. I've had it done three times, no, make that four," Maxine said. She ran a finger over the three earrings twinkling in her right earlobe. "The first time I had both ears pierced. But that seemed too ordinary, so I let one hole close up and had two more holes stuck in this one. You could do that, too, Meg."

"Whoa, let's not get carried away, here," Aunt Teddy broke in. "One hole per ear, and little studs to start out with. That's the deal."

Maxine adjusted a small mirror on the counter until she could get a good close look at her own ears. "Hmmm. Maybe I'll get a fourth hole in this ear."

"Not while I'm your chaperon you won't," Aunt Teddy said. "Besides, there's practically no place to stick another earring. Meg, we'd better keep an eye on Maxine or she'll have someone pierce her nose next!"

"Hey, great idea!" Maxine kidded back.

Meg relaxed, but only a little. Maxine ran from

counter to counter to counter, trying to find the most outrageous earrings for Meg to try on once her ears were pierced. Meg had to admit that having Aunt Teddy and Maxine along was fun. They turned everything into a big event with lots of laughs and jokes. If only her other friends could be there, too!

Meg caught the scent of strong perfume and looked up from the velvet tray of gold studs she was drooling over. A teenaged girl with a tangle of teased-out black hair and tons of makeup came up to Meg. "Hi! I'm Crystal. Getting your ears done?" she asked.

Meg whispered nervously, "I think so." Maybe this girl was the assistant to the doctor or nurse who would be doing the procedure. She looked over the girl's shoulder to see if anyone with a white lab coat was in the back of the store.

"Ready? I've got the stuff right here," Crystal said. "Let's do it fast before the store gets busy. The other person I work with didn't get here yet, and I gotta lot of earrings to unload from the stockroom."

"Here?" Meg squeaked while she looked around for her aunt and Maxine. "Isn't there some kind of room in the back where you do it?"

"Naw. What do you think this is, a hospital?" Crystal snapped her gum, then pushed Meg's hair behind her ears before Meg could say anything. "Now sit up on this stool."

Desperately, Meg tried not to feel like a toddler in a high chair who needed her mommy. How could she possibly get this thing done in front of the whole wide world? Why, there were actually two other customers in the store, one of them just a few feet away!

Before Meg could protest, Crystal took out something that looked like a small metal gun with something pointy on the end of it. Then she rubbed one of Meg's earlobes with alcohol and pulled on it.

Zing! Meg felt a prick on her ear and then a feeling of warmth.

"There, that one's done," Crystal said, blowing a bubble of gum while she swabbed rubbing alcohol on Meg's other ear.

"You mean, you pierced my ear already?" Meg said. She held onto the counter so she wouldn't fall off the stool.

"Yeah. Here comes the other one."

This time Meg didn't look at the horrible ear-piercing gun. Instead, she gazed up at the ceiling where a rounded mirror reflected the whole store. Who was that pale blonde girl who looked as if she were going to faint any second?

Unable to watch, Meg focused on a pair of tiny silver cat earrings inside the glass display case. She thought about how one day soon she, Meg Milano, could wear those very earrings, that is, if she managed not to die in the next thirty seconds.

Zing! Her other earlobe prickled, then felt warm.

"So you ready?" Maxine asked.

"I'm already done, see?" Meg answered in a shaky voice. She peeked at her ears in the mirror.

"Hooray! You did it," Maxine cried. "And I didn't hear any screams either like when I got mine done. So I figured you were still trying to decide."

Crystal looked very pleased with her victim. "I decided for her before she chickened out. I know that look. Now that'll be fifteen dollars, please."

Aunt Teddy came up and hugged Meg. "I was watching you the whole time, kiddo, and you were a real trouper. I was afraid you'd want to discuss this over and over like your mom would, so I just stayed out of sight and let Crystal handle things."

"Fifteen dollars, please," Crystal repeated impatiently.

Aunt Teddy placed a handful of bills on the counter. She, Meg, and Maxine twined arms and walked out of the Earring Fun Factory like a chorus line of happy dancers.

"Where to next?" Meg sang out. She was just positive that every shopper passing by was staring at her newly pierced ears.

"We're not going far," Aunt Teddy told Meg. "Now you need a new haircut to go with your new ears, and here's where it's going to happen."

Rock music blared out of Sassy Scissors, a hairstyling place where everyone seemed to walk out with amazing hairdos — spikes, wedges, even purple streaks. Meg and her friends had often watched kids come out of Sassy Scissors. Sometimes they wished they had the courage to go in for a haircut, but they always went back to Jeanine at Cut 'n Curl in Camden. Jeanine had been cutting their hair since they were little and still offered them lollipops at the end. Right away Meg could tell they wouldn't be giving out any lollipops at Sassy Scissors!

Aunt Teddy stepped up to the counter, where a girl or boy, Meg couldn't tell which, was on the phone. "Excuse me, we have an appointment for Meg Milano at twelve-thirty with Renee."

"Renee! Renee!" the person on the phone yelled out.

"Send her for a wash," a voice yelled back.

Wasn't Renee, whoever she was, going to look at Meg's hair before they wet it? Meg wanted to show the stylist how the sides were supposed to go and explain that the front sections had to be at least four inches long or else they curled all the way up to her forehead.

Aunt Teddy gave Meg a little push. "Go on," she said before she and Maxine sat themselves down in front of a stack of tattered fashion magazines.

Like an obedient dog, Meg followed the shampoo girl to the sinks in a small back room. There, four or five hairdressers, or maybe they were rock stars, were talking about a party they had all been to the night before.

"No, this one," the shampoo girl told Meg when she sat down in front of the wrong sink.

How were people supposed to know these things? Meg wondered. She thought about Erica Soames and Suzi Taylor, the two Know-It-All girls at her school, who got their haircuts at Sassy Scissors. They probably knew which sink to go to.

Meg lay back, and right away her neck and

shoulders ached because the chair wasn't pushed quite up to the sink. Then the shampoo girl flexed her ten long red claws and turned on the water hose. Meg shivered. The water was way too cold, but Meg didn't dare complain, especially to someone whose fingernails could put out an eye!

"Thanks," Meg mumbled when the water torture was over and her head was all wrapped up in a towel.

The shampoo girl said nothing and just pointed to the styling chair at the end of a row.

Meg climbed up and waited. She looked at her ears and wondered if everyone could tell she had just had them done. Her ears still felt a little warm, but it was worth it.

At least five long minutes passed, but still no one came. Meg wriggled in the chair. Should she go find Aunt Teddy or ask the person at the front desk for Renee? Next to her, a girl about fifteen, or possibly twenty-five, was actually getting the side of her head shaved with some kind of buzzing machine. All she needed, Meg thought, were striped pajamas and handcuffs to make her look like an escaped convict.

Meg could feel not only her ears redden, but her whole face. Suddenly she wanted to cry.

What was she doing in this place where they shaved people's heads and came at you with long claws?

Finally, finally, Aunt Teddy came to the rescue. "Renee just got back from eating her lunch. I checked. Oh, here she comes."

"Hmsh," a girl with spiky red hair said as she swallowed whatever it was she had just eaten.

"See you later, Meg," Aunt Teddy said, giving Meg's hand an encouraging squeeze.

Meg tried to act as grown-up as Aunt Teddy thought she was and sat up straight in the styling chair. "Hi," Meg said to Renee. "I just want a little cut off and . . ."

Renee showed no signs of hearing Meg and went right on unwinding the damp towel from Meg's head. "Let's see what we have here. Hard to tell. I usually like to see a client's hair when it's dry, so I can tell what it's like. I guess we'll have to make the best of it. Looks like you have some curls and waves here," the girl said, but Meg couldn't tell whether that was good or bad.

Meg tried to figure out how to tell Renee what she wanted, but before she could get another word out, Renee was ready with her deadly looking scissors. Meg coughed and tried to say something that would keep those scissors from reaching the strand of hair Renee held in her hand as if it were some sort of dead animal.

"See, even though it's sort of wavy and stuff, I wear it kind of long so it won't be so . . ."

Renee began cutting. And cutting. And cutting. Though Meg didn't get her hair cut often, she knew this wasn't going to be like Jeanine's usual trim-around-the-bottom haircut. Already long curls of hair covered the cape Meg had on. There was nothing to do but close her eyes. It was too late to do anything but sit there and pray.

As Renee's scissors clicked away, Meg felt a breeze on her neck where a lot of hair had been cut. She took a quick peek, and wondered where Meg Milano had gone. There was a girl with wildly curly hair sitting in her place!

She closed her eyes again, too scared to watch the rest of the slaughter. Maybe when she opened them again she could look for a bag or a huge Mexican *sombrero* to cover her head.

"Done!" Renee announced about twenty minutes later.

Slowly, Meg opened her eyes. Sitting before her was a girl with a gorgeous head of hair, like the coat of a fluffy spring lamb, light, pretty, and fun. In fact, now that the haircut was over, it almost seemed that there was more hair, not less, on Meg's head. All the layered cutting Renee had done had freed her beautiful hair from the weight of her old, heavy hairstyle.

"I love it," Meg said to Renee. This was the truth.

Renee studied the haircut as if it were on a mannequin and not on a real person at all. "Layering it makes it more natural. Now you have some bounce." Renee signaled Aunt Teddy to come over.

"Meggy! It's gorgeous," Aunt Teddy screamed. "It's you!"

"It's me, too!" Maxine said.

Sure enough, side by side in the mirror, Meg and Maxine had the same wild but gorgeous cloud of blonde hair.

"Don't you just love it?" Aunt Teddy asked.

"I just love it," Meg confessed. How could she not love a hairdo that made her go from being eleven to thirteen in just fifteen minutes? "I can't believe I've been trying to get my curly hair flattened for my whole life. Now my entire head is nothing but curls!"

Aunt Teddy squeezed Meg tight. "You shouldn't fight what you are. It never works, not even with hair."

8

BREAKING THE RULES

Meg sat at her desk, huddled over the very last sheet of Math Marathon problems. "I hate this, I totally hate this," she said to Marmalade who went right on licking his paw, then rubbing each of his orange ears. From downstairs, Meg could hear Laura, Molly, and Stevie having *real* fun as they helped Aunt Teddy clean up.

The Milanos were due back the next morning, and Aunt Teddy had announced that a housecleaning blitz was in order. She and Meg had spent nearly every day of the vacation on so many fun outings, that dishes, laundry, dust, and newspapers had really piled up.

Meg sighed. "I'd rather be housecleaning than

doing these math problems," she muttered. Only the thought of going to the movies in a little while made her press on.

As she stared out the window, trying to figure out the remainder of 67 divided by 3, she noticed Maxine across the way signaling her.

"Pull in the basket, Meg," Maxine called when Meg opened her window. "It's the math sheets I did. I didn't quite finish them since we're leaving for the movies any minute. But, well, I thought if the rest of you guys, well, if you put your heads together before school starts on Monday, it'd go a lot faster. Sorry I couldn't help your aunt clean up, but we got back from town late. See ya in five."

With that, Maxine slammed down the window, and Meg pulled the message basket into her room. Inside was a bulky envelope of math sheets, only half of them done. Meg noticed Maxine had left blank all the really hard problems she'd promised to do. When it came to having fun, Maxine was an A+ friend. But in the last few days Meg was beginning to agree with the rest of the girls. You couldn't always count on Maxine.

Shouts from downstairs put an end to Meg's annoyance. After all, hadn't Maxine planned one last vacation blast? They were all going to the movies tonight at the Megaplex. Meg stuffed the math sheets back into the envelope. "Twenty-two, remainder one," she said as she wrote down the answer to one last math problem.

"Uh-oh, it's Halloween again," Stevie kidded when Meg came downstairs wearing a rhinestone-studded purple sweatshirt and some red poppy-print leggings that did not match. Aunt Teddy and Maxine had convinced Meg she needed an outfit to go with her new look. Stevie, of course, disagreed.

Meg stuck out her tongue at Stevie and looked to Molly and Laura for support. All she got was a shaky smile from both of them. For days, Laura had had a hard time getting used to the new, improved Meg Milano. She couldn't help wondering whether Aunt Teddy and Maxine had lost the real Meg at the Providence Mall and come back with a different girl.

"The hair's okay, though," Stevie said. "I haven't heard you mention the word *boingy* for four whole days."

"Don't listen to her," Laura said, putting her arm through Meg's when they heard Mrs. Grant's car horn beep out front. "I love your new hairstyle." A true friend did not criticize hair. That was one of Laura's most important rules.

" 'Bye girls!'' Aunt Teddy said.

When the girls came out to the Grants' station wagon, they were surprised to see Jasmine Grant sitting in the backseat. Meg hoped Maxine and her older sister wouldn't start fighting the way they usually did when they were together. For the moment they sat silent and expressionless in the car like two strangers on a bus.

"Hurry, girls," Mrs. Grant said while she waited for everyone to climb in. "If this movie place is anything like the one we always used to go to, it'll be mobbed. Now what is it you girls want to see?"

"Milo and Otis Return," Laura said. This was a sequel to one of the Friends 4-Ever's favorite movies — the story of a stray pug and a cat who became friends.

Maxine had a different suggestion. "Let's not decide 'til we get there, okay? There's tons of other stuff playing, and we might change our minds."

"I'll let you off in front," Mrs. Grant told the girls when they finally reached the theater. "Now, Jasmine, make sure you keep an eye on the girls. I'll be back out front at nine-fifteen, okay?"

"Okay, okay," Jasmine answered as if she'd been asked to watch nursery-school toddlers.

"C'mon. Hurry up. I have to meet my friends on the ticket line, so don't take forever," she scolded.

"Isn't your mom coming?" Meg asked when Mrs. Grant's car pulled away.

"No, this is way more fun," Maxine said with a grin. "Jasmine can go off with her friends, and we can go off with ours!"

The lobby was so crowded, the long ticket lines spilled all the way out the door onto the entrance steps.

"Okay, we have to have a strategy, or I'm going to miss my movie," Jasmine ordered. "Maxine and Meg, you go on the left line, and the other girls can wait in this line. I'm going to find my friends. If we don't find each other, just wait by the ladies' room when your movie gets out. And don't get in trouble! Now get in line."

"Can't you get our tickets?" Maxine whined. "Why can't we go wait at the refreshment counter and meet you there?"

"BECAUSE I SAID SO!" Jasmine answered. She didn't seem the slightest bit embarrassed about screaming at the top of her lungs in front of all those people.

"Awright, awright," Maxine complained, grabbing Meg by the arm to go to the other long

101

line. "You don't know how lucky you are not to have sisters."

As the girls waited for their line to move ahead, which it did with the speed of a sick snail, Maxine studied the movie titles in front of them. "Too bad *Nightmare in Podville* already started. I love the *Nightmare* movies, don't you?"

Meg nodded in a way that didn't mean yes or no. She'd never seen any of the horror movies Maxine was talking about. All Meg knew was that at Halloween some of the older boys in Crispin Landing went around the neighborhood scaring everybody with horrible masks of characters from the *Nightmare* movies.

"Maxie! Maxie!" Meg heard next. When she turned around she saw four older girls from her school go up to Maxine and sneak into the line.

"Hey," a woman with two small children said to the intruders. "You have to go back to the end of the line."

One of the girls gave the woman a big fake smile. "Oh, no, our friend, Maxie, saved our places while we parked the car. It's okay."

With that, everyone but Meg started laughing and jabbing each other in the ribs as if they'd just heard the funniest joke ever. Meg waited for Maxine to introduce her to these girls, but

102

Maxine seemed to assume that if she knew them Meg must know them, too.

"So, what are you seeing, Maxie?" another one of the girls asked. "We're seeing *Deadly Force*, if there are still tickets left."

"So are we," Maxine answered much to Meg's horror. In a million years she wouldn't want to see a movie full of people falling out of glass buildings and smashing up cars the way she'd seen in the television commercials for *Deadly Force*.

"It'll be easy to get in. My older brother's friend is selling tickets on this line," one of the girls told Maxine.

"ALLTIKSFORDUDFRCESLDOUT!" a scratchy voice announced over the loudspeaker.

"Oh, no!" A groan went up from half the people in line, including Maxine and her friends.

"What did they say?" Meg asked.

"All tickets to *Deadly Force* are sold out," one of the girls complained. "Wouldn't you know it! I hope we won't have to see that dippy sequel to *Milo and Otis*. There are probably loads of tickets left for that! And it's the only thing starting soon."

Luckily for Meg, by the time she and Maxine reached the ticket counter, both *Deadly Force* and *Nightmare in Podville* had sold out.

"Sorry, girls," the teenaged ticket seller said. "Looks like it's puppy-and-kitten time for you."

"Boo hiss," Maxine joked when she plunked down her money with Meg for *Milo and Otis Return*.

"Can't you squeeze us in back of *Deadly Force*?" one of Maxine's friends pleaded. "We'll sit in the aisle. Please? My brother Andy knows you."

The boy was not impressed. "When they announce there are no more tickets, that means no more tickets. Try the next showing in two hours, and bring your parents since it's rated R. Next!"

"What a nerve!" the girl said. "I just wish my brother were here. He knows everybody, so I get to see any movie I want."

One of the girls in the group pounded on her chest like Mighty Joe Young. "Food. Me need food," she said as she pushed people aside to get to the refreshment counter.

"Phew, what a mob," Stevie complained when Meg and Maxine joined them by the soda dispenser. "Did you get tickets?"

"Yeah," Maxine complained. "To the kiddie show."

Maxine finally introduced her new friends to each other. "This is Meg and Stevie and Laura and Molly," she said, though she didn't bother

104

to mention the other girls' names. "These are some of the kids I met at Dance Craze."

"So that's why they're wearing exercise clothes to the movies," Stevie muttered to Meg. "Since when did she become 'Maxie,' anyway?"

Meg had been wondering the same thing but didn't dare ask. Maxine acted as if she'd known these new girls forever, and that she'd always been called Maxie.

"I think the movie started already," Laura announced to get everyone going. "Can't we go in? Where's your sister?"

Maxine didn't even bother to look around for Jasmine. "Jazz? Oh, she wouldn't be caught dead at a PG movie. She told me her friends got here at six-thirty to buy tickets for *Nightmare in Podville*. Boy, am I mad she wouldn't get any extras for us. Now we have to see this baby movie, instead."

It took forever for the swarm of kids now gathered with Maxine to get to the "baby movie." On the way, one of the kids in the group dropped an entire tub of popcorn on the floor and just kept right on going.

"I can't see a thing in here, can you?" Maxine asked Meg when they finally went inside the shoe box-sized theater where *Milo and Otis Return* was playing.

In the darkness, Meg saw that the audience was mainly families with little kids. Some of them were so young, their heads barely reached the top of the seats.

"There's an empty row of seats over there," Stevie told everyone until somebody yelled, "Shh! The movie's started."

The girls made their way down the row and tried not to spill their drinks and snacks. But in the darkness, Meg felt one of Maxine's friends bump into her and spill some cold soda on her back. Not much, but enough to make a cold, wet, sticky spot. Finally, finally, the girls got to their seats.

As at all the kiddie movies there was a lot of noise in the theater. A baby was crying. A little boy kept asking, "Is that Otis, Mommy? Is that Otis, Mommy?" every time the dog or the cat appeared. Kids bobbed up and down in their seats complaining they couldn't see.

This was no problem in most of Meg's row where Maxine and her friends had propped themselves on the seat backs to see the movie better. They didn't seem to realize how this blocked some of the little kids behind them.

"This is soooo boring," one of the Dance Craze girls said loudly at a particularly sweet moment when Milo and Otis were nuzzling noses on-screen. "I can't believe how dumb this is."

Comments in their row went on like this for half the movie, and soon they were followed by the hiss of angry people asking the girls to quiet down.

A few minutes later, an usher who was all of sixteen years old, came down the aisle with a flashlight. "Sit down in your seats and quiet down here," he barked down the girls' row. "Any more noise, and you're out!"

With that, he marched back up the aisle.

One of Maxine's friends wasn't about to be bossed around by a teenager in a blue uniform. "Who does he think he is, a sheriff or something in that nerdy jacket?"

The whole aisle, except for the Friends 4-Ever, hooted and stomped their feet at the sound of this. One girl even tossed up a handful of popcorn.

"I hate this," Laura whispered to Meg so Maxine couldn't hear. "I wish we'd never come."

Meg said nothing; she just sank down lower and lower into her seat so that no one would recognize her.

Meg had just gotten involved in the movie again when two beams of light shone down her aisle. "Okay, everybody in this row out! And I mean, on the double."

107

This time a much taller shadow holding a flashlight stood over the girls, and he was waving his flashlight like a police stick at the girls.

"He can't mean us," a frightened Laura whispered to a frightened Meg.

It was a nightmare in Camden, Meg thought as she made her way down the row and up the aisle. Even though it was dark, she could tell everyone in the theater was looking at her and all the other girls as the manager marched them out of the theater.

Outside, swarms of ticket holders were waiting in line for later movies. Meg hardly dared to look up, and when she did she was immediately sorry. Waiting in line were Mrs. Hansen and Mrs. Plumley, two of her favorite neighbors from Crispin Landing.

"I'm just gonna pretend that I didn't see Mrs. Hansen," Stevie muttered to everyone. "I feel like a criminal."

The only ones who didn't feel like criminals were Maxine and the girls from Dance Craze. No, they thought getting kicked out of a movie was far more fun than having to sit through it.

"Call your parents," the manager said, none too softly. "You're outta this theater for tonight, got it?"

Maxine pretended to salute. "Got it, sir." But

the man did not laugh. "Except, can I go get my sister? She's inside *Nightmare in Podville*."

The man nodded, and Maxine went off to find Jasmine. When the two sisters came out a few minutes later, Jasmine was furious.

"I can't believe you did this to me! You call Mom and Dad, and they can come and get you. Here's a quarter," Jasmine said, slapping the coin down in Maxine's hand.

"Sheesh," Maxine exclaimed. "Anybody need a ride?"

"We do, we do," her Dance Craze friends called out. "Maybe we can get your parents to drop us off at the Yellow Brick Road. It's still early!"

"Great idea!" Maxine agreed with an easy laugh.

Meg watched Maxine skip off to the pay phone with the group of girls right behind her. She knew she and the Friends 4-Ever would not be going to the Yellow Brick Road with Maxine this time.

9

HOME SWEET HOME

Aunt Teddy was a welcome sight when she came into the lobby. No matter how terrible they had been, Aunt Teddy wasn't going to scream at them the way Jasmine had in front of all the moviegoers. Still, Meg felt a fluttery feeling of shame as she, Stevie, Molly, and Laura waited at the manager's booth.

"Over here, over here," she called out to her aunt.

"These your girls?" the manager asked. "They were making a racket at the movie, and I had a lot of complaints."

Meg didn't wait for her aunt to say anything.

She knew what she had to do. "We're really sorry we wrecked the movie," she said to the man. And she *was* sorry. While she hadn't talked in the movie or blocked other people from seeing the screen, she hadn't stopped Maxine, either.

"I am, too," Laura said, right before Stevie and Molly said the same thing.

Maxine and the other girls stood on the other side of the manager's booth, just chattering away while they waited for Mrs. Grant to pick them up.

"Come on, girls," an annoyed Mrs. Grant said when she finally arrived. "Dad and I were just about to go to dinner, so you might as well come with us. Hurry along, now. I'm parked illegally out front. Sorry about this, Teddy," she called out as if nothing out of the ordinary had happened.

Not a word of apology crossed the other girls' lips. In fact, Meg could hear one of them ask Mrs. Grant if they could all go the Yellow Brick Road. When the manager saw that he had gotten all the apologies he was going to get for the evening, he walked off muttering. "Brats, what a bunch of spoiled brats."

"I know it's not your fault," Aunt Teddy said

in the car after the girls had explained what happened. "Did you get to see any of the movie?"

"A little," Meg answered miserably. "The rest of the time everybody was talking or shouting at us not to talk. Maxine was out of control like the way she was in Mr. Gleason's store."

Laura looked out the window and seemed to be talking to her reflection. "I didn't know what to say. I was thinking about all the little kids who came to have a good time at the movies, and we were wrecking it."

Molly pulled on her earring. "We should have said something to stop them, but I was afraid Maxine's friends would make fun of us."

"I thought I'd die when we saw Mrs. Hansen," Stevie said in a disgusted voice.

"Well, you learned something tonight, girls," Aunt Teddy said quietly.

What had they learned besides not to go the movies with someone nicknamed Maxie?

"Sometimes it takes a while to really find out what people are like," Aunt Teddy said, "and you often find out the hard way."

Meg looked at her aunt. "Do you know, that's just what Mom said when the Grants first moved in? I guess you two must be related after all," she said, relieved that there was something to laugh about in this whole mess. "Hey, maybe you're *not* related after all. Mom and Dad never leave the lights on when they're out."

Aunt Teddy looked just as puzzled as Meg when she pulled into the driveway. "I swear, I turned everything off but the front porch light."

"Maybe it's the monster from *Nightmare in Podville*," Stevie cackled when they all tiptoed up to the front door.

"Don't say that, Stevie," Laura said, sounding genuinely scared.

"Surprise!" two voices yelled when the door burst open before Aunt Teddy had a chance to turn the key.

"Diane! Peter! What are you doing back so soon? You weren't supposed to be here until tomorrow. Gee, I never did finish cleaning up. I wanted everything to be perfect."

"Everything is perfect," Mrs. Milano said, giving Meg a huge hug. "That is if I try not to notice that rhinestone sweatshirt and those tie-dyed pants on my daughter. I have a feeling you two went shopping without me."

"Hi, Mom," Meg said. She was half thrilled her mother was back and half worried about what her mother was going to say when she noticed Meg's pierced ears.

That only took two seconds. "Your earrings look gorgeous, honey," Mrs. Milano said. "And so does your hair."

"You mean, it's okay that I got my ears pierced?"

"It was my idea. At least after Aunt Teddy planted the idea about three months ago," Mrs. Milano joked.

Meg squeezed her mom. "Thanks."

At that moment, Marmalade woke up from his sixty-third nap of the day and finally came downstairs to greet the Milanos.

"Omigosh!" Mrs. Milano cried out. "If I didn't know Marmalade was a male cat, I'd swear he was about to have kittens. How did he get so fat in just two weeks?"

Aunt Teddy and Meg raised their eyebrows. Marmalade looked the same as ever to them — well, maybe a *little* lower to the ground now that Mrs. Milano had mentioned it.

"We gave him a cup and a half of cat kibble a day just like you wrote down, Mom," Meg said.

Mrs. Milano threw back her head. "I had a feeling you two didn't read my list too closely. It was half a cup of cat kibble a day, not *a cup and a half*, silly! Ugh, let's see if I can pick up this elephant."

Everyone but Marmalade laughed.

When Mrs. Milano put him down, her navy sweater was covered with hair. "I guess he didn't get the daily brushing I wrote down, either," she joked.

"I don't think I got a daily brushing on some days, Mom," Meg joked back.

Mrs. Milano went over to her tote bag and pulled out several small boxes and handed them out to Aunt Teddy and the girls. "I picked up a few trinkets at my dental convention. C'mon. Open them up," she urged everyone.

"Not another tooth clock, I hope," Meg groaned, rolling her eyes.

"Nope, something else. Go ahead, open it."

Meg looked inside her box and screamed. "Dangly earrings!"

Stevie, Molly, and Laura crowded around. "They're little toothbrushes!" one of the girls cried.

"Oh, Mom, they're adorable. I'll bet I'm the only girl in Rhode Island with them," Meg cried ecstatically.

"Not the only girl," Mrs. Milano answered. "I got them for Molly, and Aunt Teddy, too. I'm afraid I had to get you a toothbrush pin, Laura, since you don't have your ears pierced yet."

"Oh, I love it," Laura said, opening her box.

"Now, Stevie I had a hard time with. You're not much for earrings and jewelry, so I got something else," Mrs. Milano said with a grin.

"Hey, just what I've always wanted," Stevie said when she ripped open her box. "A pair of wind-up false teeth."

Aunt Teddy picked them up. "Let's put them on the kitchen table, and we can watch them chatter while we have some cocoa and tea."

"But first," Mrs. Milano began, "I want someone to explain a very peculiar phone call we just got from Mr. Melham right after we walked in the door."

"Mr. Melham?" Meg croaked. Did he decide to report the girls, after all?

"He said he wanted to thank you for the delicious beef stew you sent over," Mrs. Milano said, looking very puzzled along with everyone but Meg.

"Stew, yes, there was a stew about Mr. Melham, but it's all fixed now," Meg told her parents. "I'll explain later. It's a long story."

Mr. Milano began opening and closing the kitchen cupboards. "Never mind stew. Isn't there anything to eat in this place? All we had on the plane was cardboard disguised as food."

Mrs. Milano went over to the bread drawer to see if there was anything in there. She took out

116

a boxed coffee cake, then put it down when she noticed something else.

"Eeeek!" everyone heard her scream. "What are these?" She held open a rectangular plastic container of something kind of green and kind of brown.

Aunt Teddy and Meg exchanged glances. They were in trouble now, that was for sure.

"My bran muffins. You two did not eat a single one of my bran muffins," Mrs. Milano said right before she began laughing uncontrollably. "I stayed up all night to make sure you'd have something healthy for at least part of the time we were gone, and you never touched them. It's too funny."

Meg realized her parents had a good vacation without her, just as she'd had a pretty great one without them. At least most of the time.

After everyone left, she and her mother slowly walked upstairs.

"So are you and Maxine thick as thieves by now?" Mrs. Milano wanted to know.

"Not really, Mom. I'll tell you about it later," she said, giving her mother one more hug. "I'm glad you're back."

" 'Night, Meg."

When Meg went into her room, she walked to the window to see if Maxine was home yet.

But the house was completely dark. She checked if there was a note in the Hotline basket by any chance. But looking out in the moonlight, she could see that there was no note and no Hotline, either.

Sometime while they were out, the wind had blown down the Hotline rope. Now it was dangling from the side of Maxine's house. On the ground was the message basket lying in the moonlight, empty.

Meg stared at the Hotline, blowing around in the brisk night breeze. Maybe the girls would put it up again, but right then Meg wasn't sure how soon that would be.

What happens when the Friends 4-Ever spend their vacation with Laura's family in a lakeside cabin . . . and discover a mystery? *Read Friends 4-Ever #12,* FRIENDS 'TIL THE THUNDER CLAPS.

APPLE® PAPERBACKS

THE GYMNASTS™

by Elizabeth Levy